CALL ME...MAYBE

ROMANCING THE PHONE #1

MELLANIE SZERETO

Call Me…Maybe

Published by Amatoria Press
Cover art by Amatoria Press

ISBN: 978-1-942522-56-0

BOOKS BY MELLANIE SZERETO

Cowboys of Science series ~

No More Mr. Gneiss Guy

Creekside series ~

Sexy Claus

Roll With It

Already Gone

Love on the Menu series ~

Love Served Hot

Red Hot Pepper

Hot Tamale Nights (coming soon)

Love on the Menu...Extra Hot standalones ~

Just Desserts

Iced Latté

A Little Appetizer

The Main Dish

Dressing on the Side

Flavor of the Day

Love on the Menu…Steamed trilogy ~

Egging Her On

Sweetening Her Up

Reeling Her In

Love on the Menu: Steamed Boxed Set

Marry Me series ~

Mom I'd Love to Marry

Dad I'd Love to Marry

Nerd Love series ~

Comma Kaze

Nerds & Babies series ~

The Nerd Next Door

The Nerd Upstairs

The Nerd Downstairs

Nerds & Babies Boxed Set

Romancing the Phone series ~

Call Me…Maybe

Smooth Operator

Hang-Ups

Telephone Lines

Dialed Up

Mixed Messages

The Homegrown Café Book Club series ~

Makin' Bacon

The Farmer Takes a Husband

The Butcher and the Baker

When Harry Met Wally

And Baby Makes 2½

The Homegrown Café Book Club Boxed Set

The Jerk Series ~

Jerk in the Box

Jerk of All Trades

Small Town Jerk

Jerk the Ripper

Hit the Jerkpot

Hit the Road, Jerk

Two Forks Hollow Christmas short story series ~

Snowballed

Two Nights Before Christmas

Mistletoe Miscalculation

All Wrapped Up

Standalone Short Stories & Novellas ~

Behind the Mask ~ contemporary romance

Death Benefits ~ paranormal romance

Diner 49er ~ contemporary romcom

Divorce Actually ~ contemporary romcom

Frostbite ~ contemporary holiday romcom

G Marks the Spot ~ contemporary romcom

Karma-lized ~ contemporary romcom

Kiss My Sass ~ contemporary romcom

Mad About You ~ romantic suspense

Not Quite Cupid ~ contemporary romcom

With Bells On ~ contemporary romcom

You Had Me at Goodbye ~ contemporary romcom

The Sextet Anthologies ~

Volume 1: Sharing

Volume 2: Dirty Dancing

Volume 3: Occupational Hazards

Volume 4: Entanglements

Volume 5: Mistletoe & Ménage

The Sextet Presents standalones ~

Playing in the Raine: A Toy Story

Bound by Voodoo: Legends

Bewitching Desires series ~

Two if by Sea

Two Knights of Passion

Two Fated for One

Two Pirates to Treasure

Two Times the Trouble

Two Roped and Ready

Two from the Triangle

Beyond Bewitching

CHAPTER ONE

Scarlet Brinks set aside the torque wrench and grabbed the can of WD-40. After a generous squirt directed at the corroded housing bolt, she picked up the closest grease towel and wiped her hands as she faced her friend.

"If I wanted a serious relationship, I'd get a dog. Or better yet, a chicken. It could live outside, and I like eggs. They're versatile and easy to cook." Several escapees from her ponytail tangled in her eyelashes, but a swipe of her bicep brushed them away. "Look, Rose, I know you mean well, but I *only* want to get laid. Nothing more. And not like an egg. Can't you hook me up with one of your regulars? One who isn't a psycho- or sociopath, obviously."

"How am I supposed to know who's off their rocker and who isn't?" Rose Chambers wrinkled her nose and tossed Scarlet a clean shop towel. "I run a phone sex service, not mental health evaluations for potential axe murderers, although I'm pretty sure I've logged enough hours of counseling to be a psychologist. More than half the people who call just want somebody to talk to about their problems—not what I'm wearing or how I'm touching myself. Did you know my per-minute rate is cheaper than therapy? It's ridiculous. Why can't you pick up some hunk at a bar?"

"Right. Like a sexy, brainless stud is going to choose a fifty-three-year-old former rocket scientist over a twenty-something former prom queen." After a gulp of wine from her insulated travel mug, Scarlet wielded the wrench again. "You must know somebody who wants an occasional fuck-buddy. These damned hormones are driving me bananas. And my vibrator isn't getting the job done anymore. I need an actual dick."

Rose snorted and hopped down from her perch on the workbench, making the jaw-length hair on the left side of her head flop forward. The buzz-cut right side didn't budge. "I know plenty of those, my ex among them. Seriously, woman, put on a short skirt and a skimpy top, go to a bar, and let a cute young guy with a mommy complex buy you a drink. You have the body to pull it off. Perky tatas that are the genuine thing. Hourglass figure. Brains out the wazoo. Hell, I'd date you if I liked women. Spank him a few times, fuck him senseless, and send the puppy home."

"At least you noticed my brains. Most people can't get past my boobs. Oh, and puppies *follow* you home." With a massive heave, the bolt suddenly loosened and the wrench clanked onto the concrete floor, making Scarlet wince. "Maybe I need to build myself an anatomically correct AI robot, minus the usual thought processes of a man. More like a smart phone, learning from the user's behaviors."

"So, basically, a blowup doll that participates, without thinking it knows how to give you an orgasm when it doesn't." Rose tipped up her own semisweet red, straight from the single-serve bottle. "You could make a hell of a lot more money from that invention than from your second career as a mechanic. Your slogan can be 'artificial man, real orgasms.'"

Grinning over her shoulder, Scarlet caught a glimpse of their other dinner-drinks-and-dishing companion entering through the side door.

The steady click-click-click of Cerise Wethers' strappy stilettos on the garage floor announced her presence as much as her form-fitting white sundress and platinum-blonde locks laced with the most gorgeous strands of silvery gray. Lips the same color as her name and her shoes curved into a grin. "Great tagline. I'd sell them. Of course, I'd have to try out a few before they hit the shelves. My customers deserve to know what they're getting, and I deserve some nookie after a hard day's work of discussing the pros and cons of every dildo, lube, and pair of fuzzy handcuffs in the shop."

Scarlet snagged a bottle of sparkling chardonnay from the dorm fridge beside the tool cabinet where the torque wrench lived. "I'll get right on it after I finish rebuilding this rust bucket's engine for the mayor. Wine sampler? The Vinery sent over a case because I made a house call for their delivery truck yesterday."

"I'd rather have a mango martini, but it'll do. What's for supper? I'm starving. I haven't had time to eat since breakfast." Cerise balanced on her right foot while she unfastened the straps climbing partway up her left calf. "God, my feet are killing me."

"Maybe you should stop wearing hooker heels to work." The bottle hissed as Scarlet unscrewed the cap, but the ring of her friend's laughter cut it off short. A cheeky retort would undoubtedly make an appearance. "Or at least take them off when you're behind the counter. Pizza and wings are supposed to be here in about fifteen minutes."

"I'll stop wearing my hooker heels when you stop

dressing in ratty oversized shirts to hide your bodacious boobies. And those steel-toed boots have got to go." Cerise grinned and stuffed her shoes into her matching designer tote bag of a purse. "Then I'll set you up on a blind date with the cutie I hired to update the flowerbeds around the house and the shop. He seems like the kind of man who'd appreciate a great rack without being an ass about it."

"How does he feel about one-night stands? He doesn't even have to buy me dinner." Scarlet picked up her insulated mug, passed her friend the miniature bottle, and headed for the door. "Come on. I need to hop in the shower before the food gets here."

After locking up the three-bay pole barn, she trailed a high-top-clad Rose and a barefoot Cerise across the yard to her house. The lawn needed cut again from all the rain, but she'd take mud puddles and knee-high grass over snow now that almost-warm temperatures had finally arrived in north-eastern Ohio. Half a lifetime in Florida had turned her into a wintertime wimp.

Rose tapped in the code to unlock the back door and entered the garage that housed Scarlet's transportation. "Don't touch anything and take off your shoes out here. Poppy picked up four more houses to clean this month, so she doesn't have time to do yours every week."

"Yes, Mom." Scarlet unlaced her boots and then yanked her shirt over her head as she toed them off. A minute later, she dropped her grease-stained jeans and socks onto the pile. Goose bumps spread along her skin, making her nipples tighten against the thin cotton of her threadbare bra. Going without held more appeal than shopping for a new one. "Happy now?"

Shoving open the door into the kitchen, Rose scowled as

she sidestepped out of the way. "Hell, no, I'm not happy. You have three years on me and no stretch marks or Caesarean scars. Get out of my sight, you annoying old hag."

Not bothering to stifle a giggle, Scarlet trailed after her friends to the breakfast bar and then continued through the living room. "For the record, I'd rather be an annoying old hag than a dick tease. Stretch marks and scars be damned. Every guy who's ever called your hotline would fuck you in person in a heartbeat. Back in ten minutes. There's sangria in the fridge and a container of my mom's peanut butter cookies on the counter. And cut up some carrots and celery, you young whippersnappers."

Raucous laughter followed her into the master bedroom, finally fading when she closed the bathroom door. A smear of grease stood out among the flyaway hairs plastered to her forehead, but she wouldn't trade her new life for anything in the world. She'd finally made time for true friends instead of having only casual acquaintances. Her job no longer demanded sixty-hour workweeks and being on call twenty-four seven. Now she needed to find a boy-toy to satisfy her menopausal body. Wasn't her sex drive supposed to fall into a crater the size of the moon's South Pole-Aitken Basin? Instead, it had morphed into Olympus Mons.

After a quick scrub and a thorough rinse, she shut off the shower and hurried through drying to appease her suddenly growling stomach. The doorbell rang as she pulled on her clean Yes, It's Rocket Science tank top to go with a pair of yoga pants that had seen better days.

She grabbed her wallet from the organized mess on her nightstand, jogged three steps before giving up the battle of trying to corral her unbound breasts, and walked out of her bedroom. "I'll get it!"

A blurred form stood on the other side of the sidelight sheers her mom had installed within hours of discovering any stranger could peek inside her only child's new home. The discernible stack of carryout boxes assured her no Tom, peeping or otherwise, waited on the front porch.

I wouldn't be opposed to a frisky tomcat stopping by.

She raised her hand to the keypad to disarm the alarm, only to discover she'd forgotten to set the damn thing again. Her dad would have a fit if he found out she wasn't using the security system with any consistency.

The same young deliverywoman from the last three orders smiled when Scarlet opened the door. "Hey, Ms. Brinks. I have a party-size Bohemian pizza with extra mushrooms, a triple order of breadsticks with three cups of nacho cheese sauce, two dozen honey-barbecue wings, and a large order of Jo-Jos for you. You must be working on another engine."

"Hi, Emily. Yeah, the mayor would rather spend her money on a rebuild than buy a new car." Scarlet pulled a twenty from the wallet and tucked the tip in her savior's sweatshirt pocket. "I should have enough leftovers for at least a few lunches. Have you talked to your dad about wanting to become an electrician?"

An eye-roll all but confirmed the news hadn't been well received. "He wants me to try college for a year first, to see if I like it. I told him I don't need to since I already know what I want to do. He gave me *the disapproving-dad look* and said we'd talk more later, as if I'm going to change my mind. Why should I do something that's a waste of my time and his money?"

"You could try a few entrepreneur classes at the community college. Having the knowledge to run your own business would give you a leg up once you finish the trade apprenticeship you talked about last week. And your dad might be more receptive to the idea if you're thinking ahead to a few years down the road." The top container slid toward the edge of the stack balanced on Emily's arm, spurring Scarlet to relieve her of the delivery. Within two seconds, heat seeped through the bottom box and warned a quick wrap-up of the conversation was probably prudent. "Don't give up on that dream. You better get going to your next stop."

"Thanks for the advice and the tip." With a wave, Emily took off down the porch steps. "See you next time."

"Any time. Drive safely."

Instead of a half-expected over-the-shoulder frown of a know-it-all teenager, the young woman gave her a thumbs-up gesture and a smile. "You bet."

Scarlet's stomach growled much louder with the irresistible scents of barbecue sauce, garlic, and deep-fried potatoes offering immediate relief from its emptiness. "Yeah, yeah. I'm going."

By the time she reentered the kitchen, her friends had already prepared the table with paper plates and all the other necessities. A glass of sangria awaited each of them.

Cerise snagged the boxes of wings and Jo-Jos from the top of the stack and set them within reaching distance of her seat. She'd swapped her white dress for a red tank top and denim shorts, probably a wise choice given their meal. "Can I go first during the vent session?"

Rose snitched a potato wedge and dropped it on her plate. "Ouch! Hot. Which step-monsters are being bratty this time? The Hopkins hemorrhoids or the Yeats infection?"

Not bothering to hide a chuckle, Scarlet added the pizza and breadsticks to the spread. "Hemorrhoids? I thought Tony's twins were hellions."

Her twice-widowed friend picked up a sauce-drenched

boneless wing with the tongs. "They were hellions during their teens. Now they're just twenty-eight-year-old pains in my ass. Always expecting me to pay their way in life. Unfortunately, it's Margot this time. Bradley could never tell her no, and Daddy's spoiled little princess has turned into the queen bitch. She had a temper tantrum in front of a customer this morning because I wouldn't give her my car."

Rose raised an eyebrow above the rim of her glass as she tipped it up for a drink. "Why would she need to borrow your car? What happened to hers?"

"Not borrow. Have. Permanently. She totaled hers because she forgot to set the parking brake on a hill, *and* she didn't pay the last monthly insurance premium. People make blonde jokes, but that brunette uses her brain like it has the RAM of a 1986 IBM clone."

Holding a breadstick dripping cheese into the cup, Scarlet grinned. "Back when 512K was cutting edge. I remember those days. You know, no one would ever make blonde jokes to your face, especially since you're not dumb by any stretch of the imagination."

Cerise dabbed a napkin at the smear of barbecue sauce on her chin. "No, they just make smartass comments about how my husbands died. Good thing almost nobody knows about my pharmacology degrees, or they'd call me a black widow."

Rose raised her glass. "To the *blonde* widow. May she remain single forever more."

"Amen to that."

Despite her messy fingers, Scarlet scooped up her sangria-filled goblet and clinked it against her companions' matching glasses. "To being single."

Cerise's smirk promised a bawdy addition to their toast. "And to getting you an eager young fuckbuddy."

Her friends' peals of laughter nearly drowned out the ring of the doorbell.

"Gotta answer that. It's probably my dad dropping off Reginald. He and my mom are spending the weekend at the casino to celebrate their fifty-fifth wedding anniversary. Back in a sec." Stuffing half a Jo-Jo in her mouth, Scarlet pushed away from the table.

Yipping greeted her as she chewed, swallowed, and opened the door.

Her father gathered her in a hug and kissed her cheek before she could say hello. "Hiya, Lettie. How's my second-favorite girl in the whole world?"

She closed her eyes and breathed in the familiar scent of Old Spice. A dozen images from her childhood flitted through her mind as she savored the memories. "Never better. Did you tell Mom about the anniversary surprise yet?"

"Right before I came over. She's packing as we speak." He handed her a tote and then bent over to pick up the wiggling ball of brown and white fluff. "Thanks for watching Reggie for us. His food and pills are in the bag."

"Perfect. Thanks." As she reached for the fuzzy mutt, he sniffed at her mouth and then licked her chin. She grasped the leash and set her weekend roomie on the floor. "I know you're only kissing me because I smell like food, you little oinker. Have fun, Dad, and give Mom a hug for me. See you Sunday afternoon."

Reggie's yap silenced her father's response, but his smile before he headed to his car was all she needed. Life was good, even without real sex.

Snickers greeted her when she returned to the kitchen, Reggie shadowing her. "Chubby boy isn't allowed to have table scraps, so don't give in to his puppy-dog eyes."

Rose scratched the little charmer under his chin. “Cerise and I decided you should proposition the next available guy you see between the ages of twenty-one and fifty. No excuses. Deal?”

Her vaginal muscles twitched at the thought of a man-induced orgasm. Or maybe she needed to pee. “Fine. Deal.”

CHAPTER TWO

EYEING THE NUMBERS ON THE DASHBOARD CLOCK, NELSON Whitaker turned into the gravel lane leading to the sprawling brand-spanking-new brick ranch and detached three-bay garage belonging to the town's newest mechanic. Despite the early hour, a conversation with the woman sticking her nose into his daughter's education needed to happen sooner rather than later, not that eight in the morning was all that early. Any blue-collar laborer worth the time of day would be up and at 'em already, even on a Saturday—and especially to afford this house, workspace, and nearly twenty acres.

Her name was Scarlet Brinks, according to one of the guys who worked for him. She'd replaced the fuel pump in his employee's truck at a moment's notice and earned the trust of every member of his crew.

His cell rang through the speakers as he stopped in front of the smaller attached two-car garage. His foreman's name popped up on the GPS screen. *Speak of the devil.* "Whitaker here."

"Hey, boss. Just wanted to let you know the mulch is here, but we got shorted on hostas and pachysandra. The driver claimed we got what you ordered, which is bullshit of course. Then he got pissed off when I showed him the purchase order and invoice. Said to take it up with the owner. I called the place on Carpenter Street, and they have enough stock to complete the project."

Nelson swallowed a growl. "Do it. If they can't deliver, send somebody over to pick it up. The job has to be done today. I should be there by ten."

"Okay."

The line went silent, unlike the string of swear words shouting in his head. Cutting ties with a supplier ranked among his least favorite duties as head honcho of Aker's Landscaping. Why the hell couldn't people do their damn jobs?

And mind their own business.

Maybe Brinks hadn't stuck her nose into his family's personal business, but she'd offered his daughter advice without checking with him first.

He stalked to the front porch, wishing his stomach would've let him consume a second cup of coffee. This day promised to test his patience in the worst possible ways.

A shadowy form flitted past the backlit picture window to the right of the door when he mounted the first step. Before he could press the doorbell button, a thump brought his attention back to the expanse of glass. The shadow on the other side of the thin curtains became a shapely robed apparition with dark shoulder-length hair.

She dropped to the floor with her ass sticking up in the air. Then she wiggled and squirmed like she was humping someone next to the couch that blocked part of his view. Her slightly muffled voice carried through the window. "Almost. Right there. Oh my God, can you put it any deeper, Reggie? Holy shit."

Despite his previous lack of interest in and his inexperience with voyeurism, Nelson couldn't make his feet or legs move.

A sexy feminine groan followed a rumbling growl. "No, I'm not playing with your balls right now. I can't believe I got out of bed for this. Damn it, you're going on the leash."

Fairly certain confronting the mechanic wasn't such a smart idea after all, he eased away from the window and turned toward the porch steps. Maybe he could convince his six-foot-three foreman to come back with him once today's job was finished. A few beers and a game of pool might be payment enough to face off with a horny dominatrix.

The door opened behind him, making his heart lurch and the hair on his arms stand on end. He whipped back around, half expecting to see the barrel of a shotgun aimed at his chest. Instead, a fluff ball that looked like a cross between a chihuahua and a sheepdog barked and tugged at the leash hooked to its fur-hidden collar.

Her hair sticking out every which way, its barefoot owner stepped into the open doorway, right into a dribble of excitement pee. "Eww. That better not be what I think it is, mister."

The dog yapped again, twisted free of its collar, and bounded toward him.

"Reggie, heel! Sit! Stay!" She bent forward, grabbed for the furball, and stepped on the dangling end of her robe belt. The overlapping edges of fabric yanked loose, giving him a full-on frontal view of naked woman.

Holy moly. Grapefruit-sized mounds of flesh with puckered nipples generated an immediate reaction behind his zipper, not that he was usually a breast man. Four-and-a-half years without sex had evidently affected what triggered a zero-to-sixty reaction.

The corner of her mouth curved upward in unison with her eyebrow. “Take a picture. It lasts longer.”

He almost pulled his cell from his pocket to snap a few shots, but she bent to scoop up the runaway mutt still yapping at his feet. Her flowing robe flapped in a sudden gusty breeze, giving him a long peek at her bare ass and legs—his favorite parts of a woman.

She glanced up at him with a come-hither blink and a tilt of her head. “Or you could use that hard-on for its intended purpose, assuming you know what that is. Maybe you’d prefer a private lesson?”

A choked groan escaped before he could rein it in.

Crooking a finger at him, she sauntered through the open door, her robe still fluttering around her sexy calves.

He followed, determined to have the conversation that had brought him to her house. *I’m not here to get laid.* “I’m here—”

“Yes, you are. And I don’t care why.” She set the dog in a large box in the corner of the living room with at least a dozen balls, bones, and chew toys. “Amuse yourself with your toys while I do the same, Reggie.”

Nelson sighed through a frown. “I’m not a toy, and I’m here—”

“I beg to differ.” The silky midnight-blue fabric slid down one arm, revealing a toned shoulder. She grinned and let the robe puddle around her ankles.

“But—”

“Did you think about turning around or covering your eyes when my robe came untied?”

Her eyes might have stayed locked on his face, but his gaze refused to budge from the curvy form below her neck, making confirmation impossible. “No, but—”

“Are you married or in a committed relationship?”

Lying crossed his mind as he scratched at the beard stubble on his jaw. "Well, no."

"Good. Are you sexually attracted to me? Your erection says you are." She stepped closer, putting her within touching range. Then she licked her lips. "I'm not ashamed to say I'm attracted to you."

His dick hardened another notch. Since when did aggressive women do it for him? "Yes, but that doesn't mean—"

"So you'd rather suffer from blue balls than listen to your body's instincts?" Her fingertips closed around the top button of his company polo shirt. "I'm not asking you to marry me or even date me. Far from it. I just want a casual one-time encounter. You know, the one-night-stand thing men like to do, except I prefer morning sex."

He flexed his hands at his sides, trying not to think about how her boobs, her thighs, and her ass would feel.

The seductress slipped the button free and moved to the next one. "What do you say? Are you interested in sharing a pair of no-strings matching orgasms?"

His body urged him to say yes, especially when her fingers brushed his chest as she unfastened the last button, but the kind of hookup she wanted violated every piece of sex-education advice he'd given his now-adult kids.

With his heart hammering in his chest, he finally raised his gaze to hers. A million thoughts raced through his mind, among them the facts that he wasn't exactly a one-off kind of guy, his dating life sucked, and he might not have the opportunity to sleep with a woman again any time soon.

Do I say yes or don't I? "Interested? Yes. Willing? I don't know. Maybe." *Sex ed. Ah, hell.* "Do you have a condom? I don't, and no protection equals no sex. No exceptions."

She pointed toward the adjoining room and tugged him by the collar that direction while she walked backward.

"Agreed. On the counter. Have you ever had sex in a kitchen?"

The surge of relief caught him off guard. He shook his head, since the extent of his adventurous sex consisted of the hotel bed on his honeymoon over twenty years ago and only a few others after that. Even car sex didn't fall into the done-it category. Kelly hadn't let him get past first base in the front seat, even after they'd gotten married. The back seat, a living room chair, or anywhere other than a bed would've been out of the question, making this woman nothing like his late wife.

"Me neither." She stopped at the bi-level island with a quartet of barstools on the near side. "I've decided I want to have sex someplace more creative than a bed, a couch, or the floor. Being middle-aged doesn't mean everything has to be boring. If you're doing this, you need to take your pants off. Otherwise, you need to get out so I can go find fresh batteries for my vibrator."

His willpower failed him, and he let his gaze drop to her centerfold figure for the dozenth time. Would she let him watch her masturbate while he jacked off?

Damn, that would be hot, but...

Fuck it all. I'm only human.

He unbuckled his belt, hoping his kids exercised more restraint than he did when propositioned by someone so enticing, so sexy, so candid. "Just so you know, I've never done anything like this before."

Her eyes seemed focused on his zipper as he eased it downward. "I haven't, either, but I want more than a dildo can give me. Intercourse with a cock that grows and explodes. Touching. Kissing. A little foreplay would be nice. You know, to make sure I'm slippery enough."

His erection strained to get free from his underwear. God,

if the woman talked like that any more, he'd blow his load before they got started. "I can do that."

"Good."

He shoved his jeans and Jockeys past his knees and kicked off his shoes to finish the job. "I'm ready. Are you?"

"No, you're not." She slid her palms up his ribs, pushing his shirt upward and igniting a fire everywhere her skin made contact with his. "Take your shirt off. I want you naked."

Committed to his decision, he jerked his polo over his head. The snick-snick-snick of tearing cloth barely registered in his brain. He could buy another damn shirt, but a second chance to find some purely physical satisfaction with a breathtakingly hot woman might not come along a second time.

He pushed aside a momentary bout of self-consciousness, grabbed the packet from the counter, tore it open, and rolled the latex into place in record time. While he'd lost some muscle tone around the middle from too much time behind a desk over the winter, at least he still had a full head of hair. "Better?"

She sealed her lips over his without answering, which seemed to be an answer itself. Then her tongue invaded his mouth, pillaging with as much gusto as any Viking warrior, and she pressed her exquisite breasts against his chest. Somehow, her combination of assertiveness and softness made his dick harder and his heart happier.

With his hands at the backs of her upper thighs, he lifted her onto the closest barstool without making a fool of himself. Helping his crew three days a week during the busy spring season had given him respectable biceps, not that she weighed much more than a bag of fertilizer.

The padded seat put her at the perfect height to slide inside her, but he had a promise to keep first. After a slow glide of his tongue along hers, he traced her full lips and then nibbled his way to her ear and down her neck. The subtle scent of something fruity lured him along the gentle slope of her shoulder before he returned to his path to the main course.

She tightened her hold on his scalp when he licked a circuit around one taut nipple. Her breathy moan accompanied the slight sting of fingers tangled in his hair, so he circled the peak again and inched his hand higher on her toned inner thigh. She arched into him, tempting him to give her the quick version of foreplay she obviously wanted. He switched to her other breast and stalled at the edge of the dark curls between her legs. If all she wanted was a one-time hookup, he would damn well make it last more than five minutes.

Her hand closed around his wrist and pulled until his palm rested against her pubic bone. "Touch me already."

"What's your hurry?" He finally cupped her breast and sucked her nipple past his lips. A flutter of his tongue across the puckered tip earned him a gasp and a shiver that boosted his confidence in his out-of-practice skills. After another flick, he straightened to look her in the eye. "Too bad I can't take the whole day off."

Her foot crept along the back of his leg to his butt cheek. Then she hooked her calf around his waist and eliminated the space between his balls and his hand at her crotch. Her shimmy and wiggle to the very edge of the chair forced his middle finger into her slick folds. "I'm horny, I need a man-induced orgasm, and I have a long to-do list this morning. That's my hurry."

"Fair enough." Unable to resist, he rubbed his fingertip upward in search of her clit. The catch in her breath told him he'd found it. "How about if we negotiate for another longer session? A couple hours at least."

She groaned when he rubbed the swollen nub. "If it'll get you to shut up and do this, fine. Oh God, right there. More, more, more."

"Then we have a deal?" He gave her more and added a brush of his thumb over her nipple.

"Yes!" Her response might've been directly related to a sudden convulsion and the euphoric expression on her face, but damned if he wasn't going to remind her of that answer later.

Not waiting for her orgasm to subside, he guided his dick into place and slid inside her. Tremors rippled around him as he glided deeper, accelerated by the tightening of her leg at his lower back. His knees buckled from the instant head rush. "Holy fuck."

"Damn right I want a religious experience." She gripped him tighter, keeping him from losing his balance if not his mind.

The barstool wobbled as he hoisted her higher on his hips. A second later, it fell sideways into the next one in the row. He cringed at the deafening clatter and jumped backward to avoid the domino crash of metal against the floor.

His armful bounced and slammed onto his dick, hurtling him toward the point of no return. Then her body clamped around him, and her gasping cry gave him the final shove. He could only groan, hold on for dear life, and lunge for the counter while the pure pleasure of coming inside her hit him like a tidal wave.

He buried his face in her neck, trying to catch his breath and slow his hammering heart. Despite managing to land her magnificent ass on the granite surface, his legs threatened to collapse beneath him. The aroma of apple pie seemed to emanate from her hair, adding to the simultaneous floating and sinking feelings.

Her legs loosened their vise-like grip on his waist. “Wow, that was…unexpected.”

“Mm-hm.” He closed his eyes and sucked in another dessert-scented deep breath. How the hell had he gone so long without a sexual connection? Was now too soon to ask about a repeat performance? “So, I—”

Buzzing sounded from somewhere near the fridge, first in a long and steady vibration that had to be a phone call and then in three short bursts, one right after another.

The mechanic—Scarlet—grunted. “Let me up. That’s my dad’s emergency signal.”

He eased away, careful to keep the condom secure as he withdrew. A momentary pang made him wish the connection had lasted a little longer. “Want me to get it for you?”

“No.” She dropped to the floor, her legs wobbling as much as his, but he resisted reaching for her. Her noisy exhale warmed his chest as she straightened. Then she hurried to the counter between the refrigerator and the sink, giving him a long look at her gorgeous butt. “Fuck.”

His stomach twisted into a knot at her panicked tone. “Is something wrong? Can I help?”

She slouched over her cell phone and cradled her head in her hands around a pair of reading glasses she must’ve slipped on at the counter. “My mom’s on her way to the hospital.”

“What happened?” He picked up his underwear and stepped into a leg hole. His big toe caught on the fabric, sending him careening sideways into the island. “Ow. Damn it. Are you okay?”

Her shallow breaths and lack of response warned him she wasn’t anywhere near okay.

His foot now through the hole, he rushed to the counter and hauled her into his arms as she melted against him.

"Breathe. Slow and easy. Where's your bedroom? We need to get you dressed. And I'll take you to the hospital. You're in no condition to drive."

She waved toward the hall on the other side of the living room.

Abandoning his own clothes, he scooped her up and carried her in the direction she'd indicated. He clearly still wasn't a one-time kind of guy.

CHAPTER THREE

NELSON, THE MAN WHO'D FUCKED HER SENSELESS IN HER kitchen and saved the day when she'd nearly fainted, stood right outside the Emergency Department doors with his phone to his ear. He nodded for the fourth time in as many minutes, sending the overlong brown hair at the top of his head flopping onto his forehead again. The carefree hipster-dude look didn't suit his personality at all. He was uptight and responsible, despite his quick agreement to a one-morning stand.

That's not hair. It's a floppy ear, because he's a puppy. And he followed me home.

A tiny stab of guilt pricked her conscience at the overly harsh assessment. He might be cute and nice, but that didn't mean she'd changed her mind about needing a relationship. Thankfully, he hadn't mentioned the possibility of a repeat performance again during the thirty-minute drive to Cleveland. The temptation to agree to his proposition hadn't waned since the big O that had taken her by surprise, despite the fact that she'd already said yes—sort of.

Scarlet tore her gaze from him to glance at the entrance to

the exam rooms. Assurance that her mother's ambulance ride hadn't been for life-threatening reasons had done nothing to dissuade her from worrying, not that anyone had told her what had actually happened yet. Parenting parents seemed no less nerve-racking than parenting children, at least from Rose's accounts of raising two kids by herself and Cerise's experience with step-goblins.

A giant of a man in scrubs pushed through the double doors and stopped at the registration desk. After a brief exchange with the woman at the middle workstation, he stalked to the narrow opening and entered the waiting area. His lengthy stride carried him to Scarlet in six steps, close enough for her to see RN after his name. "Ms. Brinks?"

She stood, trying her damnedest not to panic. "Yes. Can I see my mom yet? Nobody'll tell me what's wrong with her. It isn't her heart, is it? You know she has a pacemaker, don't you?"

"She's going to be fine." The man's soothing words only served to increase the tension in her shoulders and jaw. He would make the perfect liar with that smooth-as-new-motor-oil voice. "The technician will be taking her for x-rays soon, so it's going to be twenty to thirty minutes before you can go back, but Mr. Brinks asked me to let you know he'll be out to see you once she's on her way to Radiology."

"*X-rays*? Did she fall?" Two hundred and six possible breaks tumbled through her mind. "I begged her to have a bone-density test a decade ago."

"It's just a precaution, ma'am. Really, she's going to be fine. Someone'll come out to get you in a little while." He fiddled with the stethoscope hanging from his almost nonexistent neck, turned toward the registration desk, and set off at a brisk walk.

Warm fingers closed around hers from behind and gave a gentle squeeze as Nelson appeared at her side. “Any news?”

“Dad’s supposed to be out shortly.” She aimed a frown at the retreating nurse’s back. “They keep saying she’s fine, but they won’t tell me what’s wrong with her or what happened. How can she be fine if they’re taking her for x-rays?”

“Maybe it’s just a precaution. It could’ve been an EKG, a CAT scan, or an MRI, which is a lot worse.” He offered a half smile and raised an eyebrow. “Did you have breakfast yet? We can make a quick run down the hall to the coffee shop while we’re waiting, if you’re hungry. You could text your dad to let him know you’ll be right back. Or I can go get something for you if you’d rather stay here.”

Her stomach took the opportunity to growl like a beast from *Mutual of Omaha’s Wild Kingdom*, nixing her inclination to refuse. “Okay, we can go, but I’m buying my own breakfast. I don’t want you getting any ideas that this is a date, because it isn’t. We’re just killing time.”

His lips twitched and his brown eyes sparkled with what appeared to be mischievousness. “Yes, ma’am. A no-strings, buy-your-own, happen-to-be-in-the-same-place meal. I promise not to ask you out or propose. I will, however, remind you of our deal at some point in the near future.”

A mini tremor in her lower belly surprised her enough to cause an almost inaudible squeak. She yanked on his hand and started toward the hallway to the food court. A long-term sexual relationship wasn’t on her shopping list any more than a romantic one. “Shut up and walk. And don’t call me ma’am. I’m not old.”

His pace matched hers as they turned into the corridor. “Of course not. What are you? Forty? Forty-two?”

“You’re joking, right? Trying to gain brownie points so I’ll have sex with you again?” She steered him toward the coffee shop line and grinned at the young man strolling past them with wide eyes and obviously nosy ears.

Nelson scrunched up his face. "Do you mind keeping your voice down?"

"Why? Are you embarrassed that you had sex with me?" She stopped at the end of the line and turned to face him. "Biological urges are perfectly natural, you know."

"No, I'm not embarrassed, but most people don't usually talk about their…" He shrugged and moved forward.

"Hookups? Dalliances? Liaisons?"

"…in public." The hint of pink on his cheeks contradicted his assertion that he wasn't ashamed, mortified, and self-conscious. "So, how old are you? Certainly not any older than me. Before you ask, I'm forty-eight."

"Youngster." Content to let him stew over that comment for a minute or ten, she stepped up to the counter and readied her credit card. "Good morning. I'd like a large regular coffee—black—and a bacon, egg, and cheese croissant."

The twenty-something woman behind the register tapped on the screen several times and then looked toward Nelson. "And what would you like, sir?"

Scarlet rolled her eyes and fought a scowl. Why did people always make assumptions? "Separate orders please. We're not together. Not like that."

"Oh, okay." After pressing her fingertip to the screen again, the young woman gestured at the card reader and announced the total. "You can run your card now."

When Scarlet completed the transaction and moved down the counter, Nelson cleared his throat. "I'll have the cranberry-walnut oatmeal and a fat-free milk."

Five minutes later, she led her puppy with his bowl of kibble and carton of milk back toward the ER. "Let me guess.

Gastrointestinal problems related to a stomach ulcer. You worry too much about what other people think of you."

He grunted. "Maybe. How old are you? If you say sixty, I'm waiting in the car."

Laughter bubbled out of her, drawing the attention of several other people in the corridor. The instantaneous reddening of his neck and ears only prolonged her amusement. She bumped his hunky bicep with her shoulder. "You should see your face. Age is just a number, you know."

"God, you *are* sixty, aren't you?" His hair fell forward like a single floppy ear again as he lowered his chin toward his chest. "My *parents* are in their sixties."

"Don't hyperventilate. Like I said, you worry way too much about unimportant things. I'm only fifty-three." She snuck a peek at his strong jawline and continued at a leisurely pace toward the waiting area. "Come on, Nelson." *Heel.*

He was quiet during the rest of the walk and stared at her when they reached the still-empty seats they'd left no more than ten minutes ago.

Dropping into the same chair, she patted the one beside her. "Sit." *Stay.*

"You don't look fifty-three." He sat and arranged his breakfast on his thigh.

It's a nice thigh, especially when it's naked. "What do you think fifty-three looks like?"

The color that had faded from his cheeks returned. "I don't know. I just remember my grandparents being in their fifties and seeming so old when I was a kid."

"You're only two years away from being in your fifties, and I can assure you I'm not a grandparent." She folded back the wrapper on her sandwich and inhaled the cheesy-salty goodness of too much fat and too many calories. She'd earned it this morning. "Or a parent, unless you count pseudo-parenting Reggie and my mom and dad on occasion. Hopefully, Reggie isn't playing Houdini for my friend like he did for me."

"Worried? I wouldn't have pegged you for—"

"No worries. Just concerned he might become dinner for one of the critters in the woods. Have you ever seen what a Cooper's hawk can do to a mourning dove? Feather explosion."

"Sounds unpleasant." He pried the lid off his oatmeal and looked past her. "Is that your dad? You have his hairline and his forehead."

Glancing across the room, she swiped a napkin over her lips as she swallowed. Her companion was right. Dad had a great hairline for an eighty-year-old man, really any age man for that matter. "Mm-hm."

Kenny Brinks' smile and jaunty gait triggered tremendous relief. He wouldn't wear his usual carefree attitude if his wife of fifty-five years had been seriously hurt.

Scarlet shoved her sandwich at Nelson and rose to greet her father with a hug. "Dad, what happened? How's Mom?"

He kissed her cheek and then held her at arm's length, his sheepish expression impossible to misread. "She's a little sore, but she'll be fine in a couple weeks or so. Just a strained muscle."

"Did she fall? You took her rollerblading again, didn't you?"

A sigh accompanied a shake of his head. His gaze dipped toward his feet and he worked his jaw. "We had a mishap this morning while we were, you know, having relations."

Choking came from behind her, but she didn't turn to check if Nelson's oatmeal had gone down the wrong pipe. She wouldn't have been able to see anyway, not past the awkward vision of her parents getting it on burned onto the back of her eyeballs. At least her dad hadn't used the word "fellatio" or "cunnilingus" this time. Mom was too sweet and motherly to have a thing for oral sex—giving or receiving—and Scarlet refused to believe otherwise.

Her parents made love—slow and easy, missionary style, at night, with the lights off.

"The doc doesn't think anything's broken. The x-rays are just in case. I was thinking we might move into that in-law suite of yours while she's recuperating." Her dad combed his fingers through his thick silver hair and looked past her. "Unless, of course, you need your privacy. Kenny Brinks. Aren't you that fella with the landscaping business? Whitcomb? No. Whitfield? Shoot! That's not right, either."

"Nelson Whitaker. Aker's Landscape Design." Nelson extended his hand, evidently recovered from her father's mention of sex. "Good to meet you, Mr. Brinks."

"Call me Kenny. Everybody does." After a vigorous handshake, her father raised a bushy eyebrow. "Do you know Scarlet personally or professionally?"

Oh my God. No. Nope. Not going there. "Dad, we're acquaintances. Nothing more. Can we get back to talking about Mom and her recuperation? You're more than welcome to stay at my house. That way you won't have to take care of her by yourself. I can set up a visiting nurse or physical therapist if she needs it. Will you please let the doctor know I'd like to discuss her aftercare? Pain medication, treatment, those kinds of things."

"Already taken care of." He peeked around her and sighed. "My daughter sometimes forgets her mother and I are grownups."

"I'm trying to be helpful." *To make up for not being here much for the last thirty-five years. And to keep you from asking too many questions.* Hoping to redirect the conversation again, she held up her coffee. "Have you eaten today? The coffee shop down the hall has a decent breakfast selection."

He waved away her offer. "We had room service before the accident. A ride back to the hotel would be great, though. We have to get our luggage and the car. Oh, and check out, even though the manager said not to worry about a thing, that she'd make sure everything was taken care of."

Given no choice but to admit she'd ridden with Nelson, which would undoubtedly spark questions she had no intention of answering, she lifted her chin. "That might be a prob—"

"It isn't a problem." Nelson handed her the sandwich and gathered his trash. "I gave Scarlet a ride to the hospital this morning since she seemed upset, but I'm happy to drive you and your wife to wherever you need to go. How about if we drop you off at her house so Mrs. Brinks can rest? Then I'll take Scarlet to the hotel and she can get your bags and drive your car back home."

I know what you're up to, mister. She shot a glare over her shoulder. "I wasn't done speaking."

He locked gazes with her for several seconds. His brown eyes held no hint of puppy-dog sorrow or self-recrimination, only what looked like determination. "I shouldn't have interrupted, but it really isn't a problem. The crew knows I won't be on site until sometime this afternoon. I'm certainly not going to leave you or your parents stranded here."

Dad patted him on the shoulder. "That's very generous of you, Nelson. We'll take you up on the offer and pay you back with dinner sometime soon. You two work out the details while I go see if my Katie-bug is done with her x-rays. Then we should be good to go."

"We'll be right here, Kenny." A self-satisfied smirk rested on Nelson's lips as he sauntered toward the closest trashcan.

So much for my first one-morning stand. Scarlet plopped into her seat and bit into her croissant, unsure how her hookup had evolved into dinner with her parents. She was still chewing when he returned. A slow sip of coffee saved her from acknowledging his presence or her pitter-pattering pulse as he sat beside her again. At least she hadn't pulled a muscle during their sexual escapade.

CHAPTER FOUR

"DAD?" EMILY WAVED HER HAND IN FRONT OF NELSON'S face. "Hey, Dad, are you in there?"

He tried to shake off the memory of Scarlet Brinks in the throes of an orgasm with a sip of lukewarm decaf. It didn't work. Every minute he'd spent with her had played over and over in his mind for the last five days, including her refusal to set a day and time for the thank-you dinner or their extended hookup—her terminology, not his. "Yeah, Em. What do you need?"

His daughter chewed on her lower lip as she pushed the remains of her scrambled eggs around her plate with a piece of toast crust. "So what do you think?"

"About what?"

She frowned and mashed the makeshift plow onto the egg crumbles. "You weren't even listening to me."

Get out of my head, Scarlet. "Sorry, I'm a little distracted this morning."

"You've been distracted all week." Her heavy sigh spoke louder than her words.

Determined to focus on the conversation, he set his mug

on the table and leaned back in his chair. "I promise to pay attention this time."

She gave him a doubtful glance and shoved away her breakfast. "I really want to be an electrician. Ms. Brinks helped me apply for the apprenticeship program yesterday after I mowed her yard."

Drawing on every ounce of his willpower, he stopped a growl before it could escape. Why did the woman have to exasperate him in every possible way? "I thought we settled this. College first, and then you can decide if you're still interested in playing with electricity."

"No, that's what *you* said was going to happen. I didn't have any say in your decision. And it's *not* playing. It's a job, one that I can start sooner than if I go to college for four years. And the training costs a lot less." She crossed her arms in front of her chest and glared at him. "I *might* be willing to take some business classes at the community college so I can run my own business someday, but my career choice isn't going to change. Just because Ry couldn't pick a major and stick to it until his junior year doesn't mean I don't know what I want to do."

Had Scarlet talked Emily into the community college idea? Maybe she didn't deserve a mind-your-own-business talk, but helping his daughter apply to electrician school had crossed a line.

Unless Em roped her into to it by saying I approve.

It wouldn't be the first time Emily had played one authority figure against another for her own gain. She'd done it since she could talk.

He braved another sip, wishing he'd watered down his coffee with ice and pint of milk. "Leave your brother out of it. I'm trying to make sure you can take care of yourself if something happens to me."

"I already do, so don't be morbid. You know, if you stopped drinking smelly mud and working seven days a week, your stomach wouldn't hate you." Her dishes in hand, his plainspoken daughter rose and stalked toward the sink. "You need to find a hobby. Or, better yet, a girlfriend."

Heat crept up his neck as she scraped, rinsed, and placed her plate in the dishwasher. Despite a strong physical attraction to Scarlet, a mechanic who propositioned strangers on her porch and influenced other people's kids without their parents' knowledge wasn't exactly his idea of girlfriend material.

He grunted to avoid slipping up about his recent un-date.

"You should go out with Ms. Brinks. Did you know she used to be a rocket scientist at NASA before she moved back to Bell? She's an aeronautical engineer. A nerd like you, except she's cool. And she's openminded about trade occupations." Em grabbed her backpack from the kitchen counter and kissed him on the cheek before she headed toward the door into the garage. "I'm studying at Meg's after graduation practice. My last final exam is tomorrow. Love you. See you later."

"Love you too. Drive carefully." The automatic response came out, even though his brain had gotten stuck on a multitude of items prior to his daughter's farewell.

One. Whether he wanted to or not, asking Scarlet on a date would result in a big fat nope. She didn't even seem all that interested in getting together for sex again.

Two. The woman was tremendously overqualified to be an auto mechanic. Hell, she could probably design the cars she fixed.

Three. Em would be graduating from high school in ten days. His baby girl wasn't little anymore.

Old enough to decide for herself what she wants to do with her life.

Oh, and she thinks I'm an uncool nerd.

He shuffled to the sink to dump the rest of his coffee. With any luck, it would clear the drain as effectively as the full-strength stuff ate his insides.

Not quite ready to tackle the landscaping bid he'd promised Cerise Wethers by the end of the week, he detoured past his office to the master bedroom—the space he'd shared with Kelly for nearly seventeen years. She might never have lived there for the lack of any reminders of her presence. Packing up what she'd left behind had been easier than it should've been. Of course, she hadn't planned to come home the day she'd died in a car crash with her secret lover anyway. The only thing that had survived the head-on collision was her suitcase full of new clothes and lingerie. How had he missed the signs?

The man in the bathroom mirror picked up the lone toothbrush in the cup and pointed it at him. "Uncool and unobservant."

Sure, they'd agreed to get married when she'd discovered she was pregnant with Ryland, though he'd planned to ask her at some point. After four years of dating, wasn't marriage and family the next logical step?

"Logical? Maybe, but still stupid. At least I have two good kids to show for it." He squeezed and bent the tube to extract the last bit of toothpaste. "And now I talk to myself for company."

Scarlet certainly came across as blunt, but she'd actually talked to him during their time in the hospital waiting area and on the drive to the hotel. She'd even given him her cell number so he could check on her mom.

God, I'm such an idiot.

He left the toothbrush hanging in his mouth to pull his phone out of his pocket. All he had to do was call her under the pretense of seeing how Katherine—Kenny's Katie-bug—was doing after their relations-related mishap. A groin injury would be so worth having somebody to love and who loved him back with all her heart.

As he scrolled for Scarlet's contact, a glob of bluish-white bubbles dripped onto his tan work shirt and oozed across the green and brown Aker's logo. *Nothing like foaming at the mouth over a woman.*

After a spit and rinse, he yanked the polo over his head, tossed it into the hamper, and tapped on her name on his way to the closet. For once, he wanted to do something unexpected, something risky. Their chemistry might spark an explosion, and not the good kind, but what-ifs wouldn't plague him for the rest of his life.

His insides squirmed and his pulse kicked up through three rings.

A grumbly sigh cut through the sudden silence. "You just interrupted my morning orgasm."

His dick twitched behind his zipper, and the spectacular image that had taunted him for five long days and four endless nights made another appearance. "If you agree to our previous arrangement, I promise to make it worth your while."

She purred into his ear. "I'm already naked."

"I can be there in eight minutes." He reached for another company shirt, willing to try for seven, even if it meant breaking the speed limit.

"Not soon enough. I've taken care of foreplay. It's time to get down to business." Her husky voice deepened another notch. "Have you ever had phone sex? Never mind. I'm ninety-nine-point-nine percent sure you haven't."

Inexperience didn't keep his trapped semi-erection from growing another inch. "Maybe not, but I can be adventurous."

Her soft chuckle skittered along his nerve endings to his balls, drawing him all in to whatever the hell she wanted. "We'll see about that. What're you wearing?"

"Jeans. Underwear. No shirt. No shoes or socks." Determined to convince her he wasn't as boring as she thought, he worked to free the button at the waistband with his right hand. Jacking off regularly since his wife's demise made him an expert, didn't it? "I'm going to put you on speaker so I can take off my pants. Then we're going to talk dirty to each other."

MENTALLY REVIEWING THE POINTERS ROSE HAD GIVEN HER over supper yesterday, Scarlet willed away her nervousness. She never should've agreed to her friend's outrageous suggestion. Oral sex—the kind that required describing sex acts over the phone—wasn't part of her skill set. Give her a glass of wine with a gathering of her new partners in menopause, and she could spout all the words that would've earned her soap in the mouth when she was a kid. Unfortunately, seven thirty in the morning was a bit too early to imbibe in the last sampler bottle and she'd only managed a few whiffs of brewing coffee.

Did guidance from a phone-sex operator give a novice an edge?

She swapped her cell for the vibrator on the counter and faced the mirror. "I'm in the bathroom so I can watch. How about you?"

Nelson cleared his throat. "I'm on my bed, but I can see

myself in the mirror above the dresser. I'd rather be watching you."

His husky admission triggered a surge of heat through her breasts and between her legs. "Like porn, do you?"

"No, I like seeing your face when you come. The moment when you tense and you feel the rush of an orgasm roaring through your body. That's the sexiest thing I've ever seen." The roughness in his voice sprinted along her spine, inciting and exciting every inch of her, from her forcefully pedicured toes to her bedhead hair.

Wondering if she sounded as breathy as she felt, she set her newest toy's vibration level to six of twelve and positioned the sonic vibrator over her clit. "So you're visual. Do you close your eyes and jack off while you remember fucking me for real? Are you doing it now?"

The words flowed much easier than she'd expected, most likely because the memory had been her own inspiration over the last several days.

He groaned, much like he had during their kitchen encounter. "Yes, right now. Every damn day. That look of absolute pleasure and those sounds you made. I can't get you out of my head. I want to suck and lick your nipples and go down on you. God, I want to taste you, Scarlet. Then I want to fuck you. For hours. And watch you come over and over with my cock inside you. I want to be inside you again so bad, feeling you pulsing around me and pulling me deeper. Until we both shatter."

An orgasm ripped through her, fueled by his succinctly expressed desires and descriptions, going on and on with the recognition that his desperation matched her own. The hoarse cries echoing off the walls changed, deepening to the low pitch of a male voice. Harsh breathing took its place as she grabbed for the bathroom counter. Her fingers connected with something that moved, followed by a *plunk* and a splash—then silence, except the buzzing from the vibrator in her other hand.

"Shit!" She lunged for the toilet, wishing she'd opted for a few sips of coffee before her morning pee. At least she'd remembered to flush, if not close the lid.

With her fingertips less than an inch from the toilet water, she stopped. Her phone rested sideways near the hole at the bottom of bowl, the screen dark from its accidental drowning.

Well, no awkward goodbye. That's a plus.

She would, however, have to make time to buy a new cell phone today after a gallon of caffeine and a shower.

And a new pair of tongs, because that's the only way I'm fishing that sucker out.

Setting aside her now-still-and-quiet toy, she trudged to the kitchen, shrugging into her robe on the way. As she retrieved a mug from the dishwasher, her landline rang.

Her pulse revved from the immediate thought that her phone-sex partner could be calling her. Before she got any crazy ideas, she stomped on the brakes. She had outgrown pubescent behavior forty years ago, the first time she'd overheard a cute boy talking about her then-C-cup boobs like they were the only part of her that mattered. Men might think with their dicks, but she used her brain.

She poured a cupful and sipped the steaming brew, the possibility of a scalded tongue be damned. A relationship wasn't part of her plan. Chemistry like theirs tended to cause explosions, fires, and a need for toxic cleanup. She'd been a witness to it on numerous occasions. "Leave a message at the beep, Nelson. Or better yet, hang up so I can drink my coffee in peace."

The recording kicked on, reciting her hours of business and instructing the caller to state their reason for calling.

"Hey, Scarlet, it's Cerise. Why aren't you answering your cell? Are you there? Pick up, or I'm setting you up on a blind date with my gardener."

She grabbed the receiver and held it to her ear, grateful she'd managed a sip of coffee. "No blind dates. I mean it."

A snort promised Cerise had no intention of listening. "The only way I'm minding my own business is if you had phone sex already, and that's highly unlikely since we just talked about it over Mai Tais and Thai food yesterday."

Prepared for a rebuttal from her second slurp, Scarlet climbed onto the closest bar stool—the one she and Nelson had knocked over during their recent in-person escapade. "Well, I did. Not fifteen minutes ago. And I accidentally knocked my phone in the toilet immediately afterward. It seems like a sign to stay the hell away from men."

Laughter forced her to hold the phone away from her ear for several long seconds. "Wait until Rose and Poppy hear that story. Who was it, and was it good for you?"

Resting her chin on her fist, Scarlet willed away a phantom uterine contraction. "The puppy."

"Really?" Cerise's one-word question promised a thorough interrogation. "Did he call you? Or did you call him? Does he have a sexy phone voice? Did you make plans to—"

"No. I'm not seeing him or talking to him again." That would be a bad idea, a very bad idea. Scarlet inhaled more fragrant steam, hoping to banish Nelson from her head. It only made her wayward brain imagine sharing coffee with him after a long night of his-and-hers orgasms. *Not good.* "I don't want him thinking I'm interested in more than sex. Because I'm not."

"So you don't want the dirty dog barking up the wrong tree? Tell me his name, and I'll fix him up with somebody who's looking for a boyfriend instead of a boy-toy."

Something that suspiciously resembled jealousy rumbled through Scarlet's insides, catching her by surprise. *Oh no, you don't.* "I can take care of him. It. The problem."

Cerise coughed. "Sure you can. What happens when you see him in the grocery store? Or at the bank? Or if he needs a mechanic? It sounds to me like you two have a steaming-hot attraction going on. Are you going to be able to keep from humping him in the produce section or the backseat of his car?"

That was a damn good question.

CHAPTER FIVE

WITH HIS JEANS BACK ON, A CLEAN SHIRT IN PLACE, AND HIS phone in his pocket, Nelson padded out of his bedroom and down the hall toward his office. Scarlet had hung up on him and she hadn't answered his text message, not surprising after he'd all but begged her for a far more intimate encounter than kitchen and phone sex. Patience was a virtue he'd sort of learned while single-parenting teenagers. Unfortunately, his gut warned him the wait would likely be long and unsuccessful. The disappointment stung more than it should have, considering he barely knew her.

A low chuckle came from behind him as he passed Ry's old bedroom. "Hey, Dad. Got a minute?"

Cold sweat formed between his shoulder blades and up his neck. His son had to have heard his conversation with Scarlet and the resulting porn sounds, even if he'd been wearing noise-canceling headphones.

Loud.

Uninhibited.

Primal.

"So…girlfriend? Or did you call one of those pay-by-the-minute services?" Ryland's teasing confirmed he'd overheard plenty and abandoned whatever he'd been doing. "I can set up a webcam for next time if you want."

Nelson continued to his desk, too intrigued by the video idea to speak for the moment. He cleared his throat as he sat and hoped his dick didn't need adjusting from its immediate interest. "What are you doing home on a Thursday? Need money for the weekend again?"

His lame attempt at deflection earned him a laugh.

Ry leaned his hip against the corner of the desk, his grin so like Nelson's he couldn't possibly be someone else's son—one of his first thoughts after discovering Kelly's treachery. "Nice try, but I'm not letting you off the hook. The washer at my apartment building is broken and I'm out of clean clothes. I figured I'd have plenty of time to do laundry before class this afternoon. You're too cheap and uptight to pay a woman to talk to you. Actually, you're not the kind of guy who would say any of the stuff you said out loud. So, who is she? How long have you been dating her?"

Despite the warmth crawling across his cheeks, Nelson powered on his laptop and banished the thought that Scarlet probably wouldn't date him if he asked. An unsettling mix of frustration and relief joined the churning half cup of coffee in his stomach. "I'm not talking about my sex life with my kids."

"Just hooking up with her then? Does she know that?" Ry's censuring tone sparked pride and something bordering on annoyance.

"How do you know *she* isn't the one who just wants to hook up?" A millisecond too late, Nelson shut his mouth. His statement held more than a grain of truth. "No, I'm not admitting to anything."

Ryland gave him a pitying look. "You like her, and all she wants is sex. Ouch."

Ouch was right, but it was more complicated than his son needed to know. "Do you mind talking about something else? Or, better yet, let me finish this quote so I can afford tuition for two college students."

"You know Em doesn't want to go to college, right? She came over and rewired my lamp and put a new plug on the sweeper a few days ago."

Finally looking up, Nelson met his son's serious gaze. "She's mentioned not being interested, but I still think she needs to at least try it."

Ry frowned. "Would you say that if it had been me who wanted to be an electrician? I get you wanting to protect her because she'd be a female working in a man's world, but you're only perpetuating the idea that women shouldn't be allowed to do manual labor jobs. Plus, she's really stubborn, which is a good thing. She'll do it with or without your approval, even though she wants your support."

"I know, Mr. Philosopher." When had his kids stopped antagonizing each other and decided to gang up on him? "She already applied to the union apprenticeship deal she told me about." *With help from my not-girlfriend.*

"Good for her." Ry's pointed stare conveyed his question before he asked it. "Did you give her a hard time for going behind your back?"

Nelson blew out a slow breath. His reaction might've been out of line, but… *But what?* "Yeah, and she called me on it. Then she said I need a hobby. Or a girlfriend."

"You seem to have an interesting new one. Girlfriend, not hobby. You could try giving her flowers and taking her to her favorite restaurant if you really like her." With an all-too-familiar smirk, Ry pushed away from the desk. "Just make sure you use a condom every time. I don't need a surprise baby sister or brother."

I deserve that after the cracks I've made about not being ready to be a grandpa. "Are you going to buy me a box, like I did for you? I'd really rather not become a father again at almost fifty."

Ry paused at the doorway and glanced over his shoulder with a wide grin. "A twelve pack or economy size? Ribbed? Lubricated? Flavored? Glow-in-the-dark? How about neon colors?"

"Geesh. I'll buy my own, thanks." Looking away, Nelson shook his head and hoped his face wasn't as red as it felt. "How do you know so much about condoms? Never mind. I don't want to know as long as you're being careful and you treat your partners with respect."

"Always. You taught me well." The grin turned into a thoughtful and disconcerting half smile. "Seriously, Dad, just be honest about how you feel. You obviously want more than phone sex and hookups with this woman, so tell her. What do you have to lose?"

"My dignity? My desire to ever try dating again?" *My new-and-improved sex life?*

Navigating to his in-progress bid file did nothing to distract Nelson from the distinct possibility he'd been dumped without ever going on a date with Scarlet. "Don't you have laundry or studying to do?"

Another step carried his son into the hallway. "I put in a load on my way in the house, and I was trying to read through tomorrow's assignments when you started telling your girlfriend what you wanted to—"

"She isn't my girlfriend." Nelson massaged his forehead, hoping his hand hid his hot face. Would Ry ever let him live down getting caught using language he'd never said to a woman before?

"But she could be if you listen to my advice." A low chuckle faded as his older child sauntered away. "Maybe I should switch my major to psychology."

Swallowing a grunt, Nelson opened the aerial maps and scanned sketches of the mini-mansion property belonging to Cerise Wethers and the building that housed Bell's first and only adult toy store. Only a handful of residents had braved protesting the permits needed to open BOB's Pleasure Palace last December, a hilarious but not surprising turnout, considering the twice-widowed blonde owned the shop. Evidently, some people still didn't believe the coroner's reports that had ruled heart-related issues as the cause of death for both of her late husbands, her choice not to change her last name for either marriage clearly an admission of guilt in their eyes.

Cerise seemed nice enough, though. She'd given him a hefty down payment, even after his insistence on submitting a detailed proposal and bid, and free reign to design a Japanese garden near the back patio and a gazebo by the duck pond. Her project was a nice break from so many generic business-sector jobs. How many different ways could he build a twenty-by-four-foot flowerbed?

His cell buzzed against the desk, sending his pulse jumping. The name on the screen brought a long moment of disappointment before he tapped the Answer icon and switched to speaker. "Good morning. Nelson Whitaker."

"Good morning, Nelson. It's Cerise Wethers. How are you?" What sounded like a car door thunked closed in the background.

Nothing like a kick in the seat of his pants to get his ass moving on this job. "Good. How are you? I'm putting your bid together right now and will send it to you this afternoon."

"No rush. I know you're not going to overcharge me or disappear partway through the job. You're an honest and reliable guy." Something jangled—keys, maybe. "The reason I called was to invite you to dinner on Sunday evening. I really appreciate the recommendations you gave me for contractors last month. Both of them did a fantastic job, and I want to thank you. Are you free at six o'clock on Sunday? How about The Vinery?"

Her breathy voice triggered a weird sensation in his gut. Was thanking him a euphemism for something else?

I need another woman thinking I'm only good for sex like I need another hole in my head.

He swallowed the frog in his throat and sat up straighter in his chair. "Like…a date?"

Please not a date. Please not a date.

Her tinkling laughter rang through the phone. "Goodness, no. I don't need that kind of trouble in my life."

Should he take that as an insult or be relieved?

Relief won, hands down. Maybe she could give some advice about how to woo Scarlet.

I did not *just use the word "woo."* His brain begged to differ. "Trouble is right."

"Once bitten, twice shy. Twice bitten, third time's most definitely a bad-luck charm."

He barked a laugh as he opened the calendar on his computer. His own twice-bitten experience remained to be seen, but it was a distinct possibility. "Sunday at The Vinery at six. I'm adding it to my schedule now."

"Perfect." A loud buzzer sounded somewhere on her end of the line. "My Thursday morning delivery's here. It's like my birthday and Christmas all rolled into one. Having new toys to unpack and record in my inventory never gets old. Talk to you soon, Nelson."

She ended the call before he could say goodbye, but hope soared through his heart at the prospect of finding a way to convince his part-time sex partner to become his girlfriend—or more than a fuckbuddy until she was ready to take the next step. Hell, a first date would be an improvement over Scarlet's bump-and-run approach.

Well, not an improvement. Just something a little less... Okay. Fine. I admit it. A little less temporary.

The realization didn't rankle as much as it should've.

"ORAL. THAT'S WHAT I MISS." POPPY GARDNER ADDED another log to the fire pit behind Cerise's house and flopped back into her collapsible canvas chair. Her red hair caught the radiance from the patio lights behind her, making it glow like a fireball. "When it's done well."

Rose refilled her wine glass and passed the empty bottle to Cerise. "Todd's—my ex's—slobber made me wetter than his skill at giving head. That's probably why he could never find my clit."

Their blonde friend shuddered and wrinkled her nose. "Gross. At least Tony and Brad didn't need a map to find my magic button. It sort of made up for them thinking I was just a pretty face and a hot body. A trophy wife."

Was Nelson good at oral? Scarlet battled against the swarm of cockroaches making her insides tickle and squirm. Despite the effort to concoct the worst possible cause for her reaction, she couldn't get the image of him smiling up at her from between her thighs out of her sex-crazed mind. At least she'd initiated the only-good-for-sex proposition with her boyfr— *Hookup.*

Poppy nudged Scarlet's knee with her foot and grinned. "Has the puppy licked your kitty yet?"

Lifting her glass to her mouth, she shook her head—not that she expected her friends to let her get away without elaborating on what she and Nelson *had* done. A gulp of mediocre chardonnay delayed the inevitable.

Rose raised an eyebrow, a clear warning another challenge was about to be issued. "Since we're living vicariously through you, your next assignment with the puppy is mutual oral sex. The infamous sixty-nine. When are you seeing him again?"

Wine snuck into Scarlet's air passage, making her eyes water as she tried not to hack up a lung. "I… I'm. Ahem. I'm not."

Cerise, who'd been unusually subdued, drilled her all-seeing gaze into Scarlet. "The gauntlet has been thrown. Unless this guy is an asshole of the first order, you're moving to the next level. Is he an asshole?"

"Of course not. He called to check on my mother, for God's sake." Embarrassment crept across her face, the heat a bit disconcerting since she'd added a hooded sweatshirt over top of her flannel shirt against the cool evening. "He seems like a considerate person, okay? But that doesn't mean I want to see him again."

Rose sat forward in her lawn chair. "Has the chemistry fizzled out already?"

Pretty sure her temperature had risen by several degrees, Scarlet slumped against the back of the glider. "No, but…"

A muffled *pop* from the direction of the bar under the second-story deck drew Scarlet's attention to Cerise. Her friend strolled in a wobbly line toward the fire, a new bottle in her hand. "If she doesn't want to hook up with the puppy again, then we'll find another prospect. Who's ready for a taste of Tony's prized 1994 Château Chienne? Or whatever it's called. Doesn't *chienne* mean female dog in French?"

Thankful for the diversion, Scarlet drained her glass. "I think so. I'm ready. What makes this one so special?"

"I have no idea. Maybe because it's made at the bitch castle? Thus, the name. That can't be a bad thing, can it?" The soft *glug*, *glug*, *glug* of deep red liquid as Cerise poured blended with the soothing crackle of the fire. "He's probably rolling over in his grave tonight because I raided the wine cellar. Serves him right for dying and leaving his precious collection to me."

Giggles erupted around their cozy gathering. Husband number one had left investments they couldn't touch for years to his adult children. Everything else, including his collectibles, had gone to trophy wife number four—Cerise, the only woman who hadn't cheated on him.

Poppy dumped the remains of the meh-tasting chardonnay in the grass and raised her stemless glass. "Rolling is good. Dinner rolls. Rollers for your hair. Not the Rolling Stones, though. I prefer Bob Seger and Boston. Ooh. Definitely a roll in the hay."

More laughter echoed across the manicured backyard, almost making Scarlet forget the mishap with her phone that morning and the text waiting for her when she'd activated her new cell. A sip of the cabernet chased away the memories with the urge to spit the dry-as-a-desert wine back into her glass and mix it with the chardonnay on the ground. "Ew, that's nasty. I don't suppose Tony left you any hundred-year-old Scotch or some vintage Portuguese rum? You know, something drinkable."

Cerise handed the bottle to Poppy as she dropped into her seat. "Several cases of vodka, but I drank it all within the first year after Brad made his grand escape from Margot. Lucky bastard. I want to die while I'm having an orgasm, preferably while Scar's AI guy has his head between my thighs."

Rose's raspberry created a sound effect for the spray of wine from Poppy's mouth. Their host choked and spent the next several minutes coughing in between hysterical laughter.

With a sly smile, Cerise tossed the expensive cabernet into the fire, sparking flames resembling a solar flare. "So, back to the oral sex challenge. We need to map out a plan, Scarlet. How about if we have dinner at The Vinery Sunday evening? Does six o'clock work for you?"

CHAPTER SIX

SCANNING FOR CERISE'S AUDI AS SHE HEADED ACROSS THE parking lot, Scarlet hoped her feet withstood the walk to their table in three-inch heels. Almost a year had passed since she'd worn pumps instead of work boots, tennis shoes, or flip-flops. At least she'd had the foresight not to wear a skirt and pantyhose. Dress pants and a top that did nothing to minimize the size of her breasts weren't much better, especially when she could've been lounging around in sweats. The outfit would, however, appease her friend's penchant for wanting her to show off her assets.

Not surprisingly, the champagne-colored R8 was nowhere to be seen since Cerise had sent a text message that she might be a few minutes late. If she was smart, she'd chosen to enjoy a few minutes alone with the toy samples her suppliers sent when new models released.

At the entrance to the winery's restaurant, Scarlet returned the porter's smile and greeting, despite his use of ma'am and her reluctance to let her friends bully her into searching for an orally gifted man. As much as she'd love to be licked like a lollipop until her center matched the gooey consistency of a melty Tootsie Roll, the chances of finding a skilled licker seemed as likely as winning the lottery.

The hostess smiled as Scarlet approached the podium. "Good evening. Do you have a reservation?"

Giving a nod, Scarlet tried to clear her mind of men and oral pleasure. "Yes, I'm meeting a friend. Cer—"

Someone bumped into her back, and a hand grasped her shoulder, steadying her on her wobbly heels. "Oops, sorry. I wasn't paying atten— Scarlet?"

The tentative question sparked an unexpected jolt in her lower belly. After a moment to catch her balance, she turned away from the greeter and to the man standing behind her. "Nelson. Hi."

Geesh, could she have sounded any breathier?

His lips formed a slight frown and his eyebrows scrunched downward, suggesting he wasn't exactly pleased to see her. "Hi."

Was he on a date?

Her stomach tensed. *I am not jealous. And it's none of my business.*

See? This is why I have no interest in a relationship.

She cleared her throat and grabbed at the first thought in her head. "I dropped—" *He doesn't need to hear that story.* "My phone died Thursday morning. I had to buy a new one at lunchtime."

His mouth and the lines around his eyes softened. Then a hint of a pleased smile appeared. "So, you didn't hang up on me?"

Her brain misfiring from the change in his expression, she shrugged and tried to regain some semblance of control over her haywire hormones. "Technically speaking, yes. But it was an accident. Are you here for dinner?"

No, he's here for a haircut and shave.

"Yes, I'm meeting a client." He glanced toward the dining room and back again. "I don't think she's here yet, if you have a minute to talk."

She clutched her purse tighter instead of pressing on her stomach to calm her misbehaving insides. "I'm meeting a friend, but she texted that she's going to be a little late."

"Good. Well, not necessarily good, but…" With a sigh, he nodded toward the hostess stand. "Do you mind if I join you at your table until your friend gets here?"

"I… Of course not." Turning back to the young woman, Scarlet willed her brain and her mouth to cooperate with each other. "Sorry for the interruption. As I started to say, Cerise Wethers has a reservation for two at six o'clock."

The hostess picked up two menus and gestured toward the entrance to the private balcony seating. "Right this way, Ms. Brinks. Mr. Whitaker."

Nelson's low snicker sent a warm tingle down her spine, but Scarlet followed their guide. A disconcerting feeling joined it, and she waited until he held her chair and she sat before narrowing her gaze at him.

The young woman smiled again and set the menus on the table at each place setting. "Your server will be right out to take your drink order and tell you about tonight's specials."

Amusement glinted in her companion's suddenly welcoming eyes, but he sat silently until the greeter left. "I think we've been set up. Cerise is the client I was supposed to have dinner with. She wanted to thank me for some contractor recommendations I gave her and to talk about my landscaping bid for her shop and the estate."

Shaking her head, Scarlet tried—unsuccessfully—to ignore the elation flooding her body. She should be thoroughly pissed off at her friend for arranging a blind date, not looking forward to spending the next two to three hours—

fully clothed—with the man she'd been referring to as her puppy. "I should've seen this coming."

"Does Cerise arrange blind dates for you often?" His grip on the menu tightened a fraction.

Hmm... Is he jealous or just possessive of someone he isn't even dating? She nearly barked a laugh. Nelson was no alpha, let alone an alpha asshole. "No, but she's tried. This is the first time she's done it without my consent."

"You're not mad, are you? You'll stay and have dinner with me?" His hopeful expression smothered the sudden panicked urge to go home and order a pizza. "If Cerise didn't make arrangements to pick up the tab, I'm happy to pay. I'd like to get to know you better. Socially. Intellectually."

"Oh, she's paying, whether she planned to or not. Literally and figuratively." Turning her attention to the menu, Scarlet grinned. "Do you know any single men who have a thing for blondes and adult toys?"

SCARLET BRINKS WAS BLUNT, BRILLIANT, AND BEAUTIFUL, not to mention sexy as sin in her reading glasses. Nelson had no hope of fighting the feelings that had morphed from strong sexual attraction, animosity, and tentative romantic interest to intense sexual attraction, respect, unabashed affection, and a lot of other emotions he couldn't quite define yet. Nothing about her was fake, and he couldn't deny the revelation buzzing in his head as she sat back in her chair after eating an entire plate of shrimp and goat cheese primavera, two rolls, a side salad, and half the apple dumpling a la mode they'd shared.

He'd taken an unexpectedly huge step toward falling in love with this contrary yet sexy woman in the last two hours.

Conversation had been easy. She hadn't freaked out when he'd made a few casual mentions of having grown children, and they'd already proven beyond a shadow of a doubt they were sexually compatible.

No, he hadn't really planned on looking for a serious relationship, especially one that started out strictly physical, now that his kids had turned into partially independent adults. His business needed his attention, but Ry and Em were right about finding a hobby or a girlfriend. He deserved something that brought balance and enjoyment to his life. His kids might even quit badgering him about getting a social life.

"You look like you're deep in thought." Scarlet dabbed at her kissable lips and then set her napkin on the table beside her empty wine glass. "Or you're in a food coma."

"Both. I'm a decent cook, but I haven't had a meal this good in a long time." Taking a calming breath, he steeled himself for an honest discussion about their future. "And the company has been…exceptional. In fact, I'd like to see you again—for a date we've agreed to, that wasn't arranged by someone else. If you're interested."

Her gaze had never left his as he'd spoken, but her eyebrows had risen when he'd suggested a repeat of tonight. Still, she stared right at him, whatever thoughts going on in her head unreadable. "A real date. Without sex?"

Telltale warmth flushed his cheeks as their server appeared behind Scarlet. He stayed silent until the waiter informed them Cerise had taken care of the bill, cleared the remaining dishes, and headed back into the main dining room.

The extra time didn't help him formulate a response. He'd have to wing it. "Not necessarily. I just want to do other things too. I like talking to you and spending time with you when we're wearing clothes."

Her mouth curved upward the tiniest bit, but the sparkle in her eyes confirmed her amusement. "Well, if sex is still on the table, a date might be okay."

On the table, the floor, the couch, the bed—he wouldn't be opposed to any of those options. "It is."

"Three times a week? I have needs, you know." Her smile widened into a decidedly wicked smirk, setting off a twinge behind his zipper and a warning signal about her negotiation skills when she wasn't under the influence of an impending orgasm.

The chance to take care of her needs every other day almost lured him into agreeing to her terms without further discussion. "As long as they all involve an activity that isn't sex-related. A movie, a hike, cooking dinner together, that kind of stuff. So we can get to know each other better. With our clothes on."

She sighed, but the grin never left her face. "I guess I don't have a choice since you've already met my parents."

"You always have a choice." He stood and held out his hand, hoping for a touch. "You can tell me no or you can tell me yes. If you want to think about it, that's fine too."

Her fingers wove themselves with his as she rose. Then she leaned close enough to tickle his ear with her breath. "What if I want to choose the sexual position?"

He nearly choked on his own saliva, and his dick pressing against the front of his pants tempted him to die a happy man right then and there with an audience. How did she do that to him—a normally inhibited guy with very vanilla experience in the sex department? "I'm okay with that. My house or yours?"

The wicked gleam returned to her eyes as she met his gaze. "How about in your truck out at the lake behind my house? I have a bunch of moving pads in my garage. We can toss a few in the back. As long as Mom and Dad aren't out on the deck, nobody should hear us."

With a curt nod, he let her lead him toward the front of the restaurant. The woman could probably convince him to rob a bank for the promise of a quickie—and he wouldn't even regret the jailtime if he got caught. Had he ever been this energized and aroused by his late almost-ex-wife?

That would be a most definite no.

Scarlet thanked the porter when he pushed open the door for them and then she aimed for the far corner of the parking lot, her high heels clicking on the pavement. Were they left-overs from her career as a rocket scientist?

The setting sun cast a fiery hue on her loose hair, warning him getting burned was a very real possibility, but he couldn't convince his heart or his brain to care. She brought excitement and adventure to his boring life.

"You've never had outdoor sex before, have you?" She stopped at the rear bumper of the vivid blue Aston Martin a few spots down from where he'd parked. "I'm in the mood to try something new."

Retrieving his keys from his pocket, he cocked his head to the right. "I think you already know the answer to that question. Where are you parked? I'll follow you."

Her lips curved upward again and she brushed her fingertips along the backend of the sporty import. "Right here. She's a beauty, isn't she?"

He nodded, too aware of the fact that she'd probably paid more for the car than he'd spent on his house. God, the woman was so far out of his league. "Good thing I know where you live. I'm not sure my truck will keep up with your race car."

She tipped her head back as she laughed, a sound so genuine he barely kept from hauling her into his arms and kissing her until they couldn't breathe. "I promise to obey the speed limit. If you're good, I'll take you for a ride sometime."

Watching her slide into the car, he tried to strangle the feeling that she might already be taking him for a ride. While he'd never been a use-'em-and-lose-'em guy, some of his male acquaintances in high school and college had employed that philosophy, and women weren't all that different. His marriage had taught him that hard lesson.

He trudged to his truck with his heart somehow finding room to sink into his full stomach. Teenage angst didn't belong in the realm of middle-aged dating. Navigating a social life already challenged him enough.

True to her word, Scarlet drove at a sedate speed out of the parking lot, past the rolling hills lined with row after row of grapevines, and along the country roads leading toward Bell. She hugged the curves, reminding him of the personal details she'd shared during dinner about growing up in the little town and how her mom had taught her to drive at fourteen on the same backroads. Those stories had drawn him in and given him hope that she might be open to a real relationship.

He made the turn into her driveway behind her and stopped in front of the garage. Regardless of the relaxed drive to her house, his emotions had suffered whiplash during the eleven-minute trip.

She raised her index finger at him as she exited her car and then disappeared past the second overhead door. As she reappeared a few minutes later with a load of neatly folded moving pads, a ball of brown and white fluff raced across the sidewalk and into the garage. Yapping carried through the truck window while Reggie the escape artist circled her feet.

Pretty sure she needed assistance, Nelson climbed out of his truck and slowly approached the dog. "Reggie, sit."

The critter yapped twice and took off like a bat out of hell toward the front yard.

"I'll go this way." He pointed in the direction Reggie had gone. "You go around the other way. Maybe we can catch him in the middle."

Giving a nod, she kicked off her heels and tossed aside her armful. Then she darted toward the smaller entry door at the back of the garage.

More barking led Nelson past the porch and around a barren flowerbed at the far end of the house. As he reached the next corner, the raggedy mutt ran toward the tree line about fifty yards beyond the multi-level deck. An abandoned dog treat on the railing caught Nelson's eye.

He detoured to his best chance of capturing the escapee. "Biscuit! Num-num! Come get a treat, Reggie! Who's a good boy?"

Reggie skidded to a stop and looked toward the house.

"Come on, Reggie! Get your biscuit!" Holding out the bone-shaped treat, Nelson squatted and patted the ground. "Good boy, Reggie. Come and get it."

After several antsy steps, the furball glanced into the woods and dropped onto his belly.

Heavy footsteps came from behind Nelson and then a pair of grease-stained steel-toed boots moved into his peripheral vision.

Scarlet tromped closer and perched her fists on her hips. "Suppertime, Reginald!"

The dog yapped again as he popped up from the ground. Then he shot into the woods.

"Damn it!" With a growl, she set off at a fast-paced jog in her work boots and switched to speed-walking half a dozen steps across the weedy yard. "Stupid boobs. Stay here in case he comes back."

Nelson bit his lower lip to keep from grinning, not that her departure or approaching dusk gave her much chance to notice his amusement. Her breasts were perfect, even if they bounced when she ran.

Another round of barking started as soon as she entered the line of trees.

He kept his attention on the spot and prepared to dodge left or right if the dog suddenly appeared. Within a minute, his phone buzzed in his pocket.

Caught between annoyance at the distraction and concern that Ry or Em needed him, he pulled out his cell. The screen darkened a moment after Scarlet's name stood out above the text. Her message, "*Dad's hurt*," made him spring into action and follow the path she'd taken.

And the Lassie Timmy-fell-in-the-well Award goes to Sir Reginald Brinks.

CHAPTER SEVEN

"STRAINED MUSCLES AND TWISTED ANKLES. I NEED TO INVEST in bubble wrap and buy a lifetime supply for my parents." Scarlet leaned back in the lounge chair on Rose's patio and focused on the clear evening sky. It did little to distract her thoughts from last night's trip to the emergency room with her father and Nelson's generous offer to stay with her mom while Scarlet handled her second trip to the hospital in less than two weeks. He'd practically carried her dad from the woods to her SUV, managed to corral Reggie into the in-law suite, played and lost four games of Scrabble with her mother during their at-home wait, helped her dad back into the house, and made sure the doors were locked on his way out at 1:00 a.m.—after not having sex with her.

Tomorrow can't get here soon enough.

Rose flipped the burgers on the grill, making them sizzle and filling the air with mouthwatering wisps of meat-scented smoke as Poppy slipped into the house to retrieve the potato salad from the fridge. "I guess that means the oral sex challenge didn't work out the way Cerise planned."

"That would be a big fat nope. She told you about the bait

and switch at The Vinery, huh?" Not quite ready to let her friends in on the secret that blind-date guy and the puppy were one and the same, Scarlet frowned. "Good thing she can't make it tonight, because I'm still a little miffed she had the balls to set me up, especially when she knew I already had a plan for Project #69."

A snicker accompanied another noisy sizzle from their supper. "After the fact, but, yeah, she mentioned it this afternoon when she called. Planning some payback? Muenster, baby Swiss, or Colby on your hamburger?"

"Muenster. I'm thinking we should suggest she hire a studly security guard to stay at the shop with her when she's working afterhours. Then, oops! The security system accidentally locks them inside together for the night." Scarlet cracked her knuckles and wiggled her fingers in the air. "I bet I can work some magic so that it goes on lockdown if she pushes any button. With a nearly unlimited supply of condoms, hundreds of toys, and one hot and hard dick, I bet her clothes will fall off within the first five minutes."

Rose's hoot of laughter frightened a rabbit at the edge of the field into hiding under the shrubs. "Remind me not to piss you off."

"What's the matter?" Tossing her friend a grin, Scarlet sat up, in hopes their supper was almost ready. "Don't you want to have sweaty sex with more than a voice on the phone?"

"Hey, at least with phone sex I know I'll get an orgasm out of it if I want one. The real thing, not so much."

"Mm-mm-mm. Looks like I'm just in time for food and raunchy conversation." A woman with sleek jet-black hair clicked her way toward the patio in flip-flops, a grocery bag balanced in one arm. "Thanks for the invite, Rosie. You need a trim. The stubble side's getting a little stabby-looking."

Still wielding the greasy burger flipper, Rose pointed to

the round umbrella table a few feet from Scarlet's lounge chair. "Glad you could come. Squeeze me in for a shave this week if you can. Cookies and chips can go on the table. Sienna, Scarlet. Scarlet, Sienna. Sienna's been cutting my hair forever and just opened Whacked next door to BOB's. She went to high school with Poppy and me a hundred years ago and moved to Bell last weekend. Scarlet runs the auto repair shop outside of town."

Scarlet stood and nodded at the new guest. "Good to meet you, Sienna. If you like blunt talk about sex, menopause, and dicks, you'll feel right at home."

The woman's smile grew as she raised her sunglasses and pushed them into her glossy black hair. "Yep, but not necessarily in that order. Menopause is a pain in the ass, and sex and dicks fall into the category of you can't live with it and you can't live without it. Rose said you're inventing a fuck-buddy robot. Any idea how soon it'll be ready?"

With another whiff of burger, Scarlet opened the package of buns. "It's still in the idea stage. Are you volunteering for the performance assessment team?"

"You betcha." Their dinner companion placed her contributions to the cookout next to the assortment of condiments and toppings and then popped the lid off a square container. "Brownie? I made the good kind."

Poppy snickered as she stepped through the patio door. "With pot?"

Sienna's eyes widened and her jaw dropped, but her shoulders shook like she could barely contain her amusement. "Triple fudge. I can't believe you said that, Poppyseed. You've always been such a bad influence on me."

"Yeah, right." Their redheaded friend set the bowl of potato salad in an empty spot. "Says the person who mooned the principal after the senior night football game."

"Twenty-five years ago." The pickle jar popped when Sienna twisted the lid. "God, no, it was over thirty now. When did we get old?"

Filling the first of four glasses from the insulated gallon jug, Scarlet raised an eyebrow at Sienna and then Poppy. "Who's old? Sure as hell not me. Want a drink? Coconut rum and vodka mixed with cream soda, cranberry juice, and a dash of whipping cream."

Rose transferred the last burger to a platter and added the main dish to the table. "I think we should call it the creamy tart. Two of those, and you'll be horny enough to sleep with any guy who's sporting a boner. Of course I want it."

Wearing a wide grin, Poppy nodded. "Me too. I like that. The name, not the prospect of having sex with just any guy. Speaking of which, how's the pup, Scar? Or did you trade him for oral-sex guy?"

Sienna's eyebrows rose almost to her hairline. "You have two men? One for oral and one for intercourse? I think you need to share. And pour one of those for me."

Heat crawled up Scarlet's neck as she served up a round of creamy tarts. Despite her raging sex drive, the thought of two male mouths held no appeal—unless she could keep them from talking. "One. He's one person, and I…" She sighed. "I might kinda, sorta like him, okay? Last night's blind date was also phone-sex and kitchen-sex guy."

With the glass an inch from her lips, Poppy froze. "No kidding?"

The flipper clattered against the tray and Rose's mouth hung open. "The puppy is Cerise's landscaper? Nelson Whitaker? My daughter Meg's best friend's dad? The poor man whose cheating wife died in a car accident with her lover when she was leaving him and their kids without so much as a note? That landscaper?"

Scarlet's heart fell to her empty stomach, where her phone suddenly buzzed against the roiling beast. Taking advantage of the distraction, she pulled her cell from her sweatshirt pocket and opened her messages. Nelson's name topped the column of texts.

"How are your mom and dad doing today? Can't wait to see you tomorrow."

Her heart fluttered back up to its normal location, making her lightheaded. "Um, yes, he's a landscape architect. I figured he was divorced. Wow. What kind of person does that to their spouse? And their children?"

Rose guided her to the lounge chair. "I'd say karma decided a dead one fit the bill. He's a good guy. Clearly not as uptight as I thought he was since he's been taking care of that sex-crazed libido of yours. Sit. You look like you're about to fall down."

"He just texted to ask about my parents again. And to say he's looking forward to the next time we see each other." Scarlet plopped on the chaise and cradled her head in her hands, cursing the damn angsty feelings coursing through her body. "This was *not* supposed to happen. I wanted sex. A boy toy. Not a boyfriend. Is that even the right word when you're in your fifties?"

"It depends on how you responded to his message." Curiosity colored Rose's words, and she rubbed the tense knots between Scarlet's shoulder blades with her thumbs. "How do you feel about him? It's okay if you like him, you know. Being cautious is fine, but we're not man-haters. And you could do a lot worse."

"It's just that I was having fun treating men like sex objects since that's the way they've treated me my entire life. A lot of them anyway. The rest act like I'm a bitch because I'm smart, like I'm threatening their stupid masculinity or something." That wasn't entirely true, at least not where Nelson was concerned. "He's different, and I don't know how to… I just don't know."

Poppy sat on the end of the lounge chair and lifted Scarlet's bare feet onto her lap. "What did his text say and how do you want to answer?"

She reopened the message and read it aloud. "We have a date tomorrow. A real one. He's making me dinner at his house and we're supposed to have sex. That was our negotiated agreement. I wanted sex three times a week and he said he'd agree if we also did the dating kind of stuff. Then, last night when he left, he gave me a hug and a kiss. Not like *let's go have sex*. Like *I care about you and I want to take care of you*. I wanted him to stay, even though I was too exhausted to get naked with him. No man has ever acted like he wanted to take care of me, except my dad."

Scraping a lawn chair closer, Sienna handed her a creamy tart. "He sounds like a nice guy. Are you excited to see him tomorrow? Racing heart, somersaulting stomach, can't stop thinking about him?"

A gulp of opaque pink cocktail did nothing to calm Scarlet's symptoms. She nodded. "The last time I felt this way was when my team designed and built a piece of equipment that went to the space station. I don't like feeling this way about a man."

A trio of giggles broke a long moment of silence, and Sienna turned toward the table. "Tell him the truth—that you're looking forward to seeing him too. Whether you want a relationship or not, he deserves to suffer from that giddy feeling as much as you do. What do you want on your burger?"

❧

"I'm going to Meg's after work and staying the night so we can finish making decorations for the graduation party." Emily peeked in the crockpot and inhaled. "Oh, man, you made pulled pork for supper? Not fair. What? You have a hot date tonight? Probably just the crew so you can talk about work."

Shoving his head into the fridge to hide his no-doubt lovesick expression, he grabbed the corn on the cob. "As a matter of fact, I do have a date."

"Wow. No kidding? Like a real date? With a woman who isn't a client or a business contact?" Her voice moved closer, as did her footsteps, and her feet appeared behind him as he closed the vegetable drawer.

Without turning toward her, he stepped to the sink. "Yes, a real date."

"Who is she? Where'd you meet her?" A gasp followed his daughter's short silence. "Ry said he overheard you having phone sex—"

"Stop." *Note to self—embarrass my children as often as possible in front of their kids.* "If you value your place in my will, you won't ever say another word about what your brother told you. Ever. Even when I'm dead."

Her first cackle became a second and then full-blown cracking up as she grabbed for the counter. She missed and ended up in a watery-eyed, gasping heap on the floor. "At least... At least she can't get...pregnant over the phone!"

More howling laughter brought a blast of scorching heat to his neck and face. As horrifying as having his kids know he'd engaged in phone sex, he didn't regret a moment of the time he'd spent with Scarlet—naked or otherwise.

"Shouldn't you be leaving for work?" He blew out a heavy sigh and peeled the top layer of leaves partway down the first cob while Em caught her breath.

She stood and peeked around him with a wide grin. "No more teasing, I promise. I think it's great that you found a girlfriend and you're having fun. I'll text you when I get to Meg's."

His skin finally cooled. "Okay. Drive carefully. I love you."

"Of course. Love you too, Dad." After a quick peck on his cheek, she hurried across the kitchen. "Don't forget to use a condom."

The hum of the garage door opener followed the clunk of the door closing, leaving him alone to stew in his mortification and nervousness. The rain pattering against the window over the sink only added to his edginess, especially since two big projects needed to be finished by the end of the week.

His phone buzzed against the counter, sending his pulse skyrocketing again, but the number belonged to his foreman. "What now?"

After a tap on the Answer button and switching to speaker, he returned to partially shucking the corn. "Whitaker here."

"Hey, boss. I just wanted to catch you up to speed. Simon Cortez called this morning to let me know the first four model homes were ready for interior staging, so I put both crews to work on the planters and placement of the potted plants. We finished up about ten minutes ago."

A fraction of the tension in his shoulders and neck eased. "Perfect timing. That means we can move up the start date for the Wethers commercial project to Monday if the rain stays south. You like the new supplier? No shortages?"

"Everything matches the purchase order unless they've notified us ahead of time. Best service of anybody we've used in twenty years."

"That's what I like to hear. I'll see what I can do about

negotiating a longer-term contract with them." Done removing the silk from both ears, he folded the leaves back into place.

"Sounds good." A pair of high-pitched squeals drowned out whatever his foreman said next. "Hang on a sec, girls. Let me say goodbye."

Caught between missing the days when his kids ran to the door to greet him and glad not to be parenting young children alone, Nelson shook his head. "You must be home. Tell the family I said hi."

"Will do. See you in the morning."

The phone went silent as he herded the last few stubborn strands of corn silk off the counter and into the trash. After a quick check of the clock, he set the table and gave up any pretense of being patient to go watch for Scarlet at the living room window.

Heavy rain pelted the pavement, creating a fast-moving stream at the end of his driveway. A set of headlights cut through the wall of dreariness and a turn signal blinked on the right corner of the SUV, shooting his pulse into high gear again.

Not waiting to see where the vehicle was turning, he jogged to the garage and tapped the opener. As the door to Em's side rose, light and raindrops snuck through the widening gap at the bottom. The headlights and rain barely allowed him a peek at Scarlet through the rapid swipes across her drenched windshield, but his body—his heart every bit as much as his dick—recognized her and responded anyway.

Breathe.

He waved her into the empty space, impatient to pull her into his arms and lose himself in a kiss.

Her gaze met his when she shut off the engine, and a sly grin formed when he pressed the button again to close out the weather and the world. Still looking straight at him, she climbed out. “Does this mean we have the house to ourselves?”

Stunned by the desire in her eyes, he nodded.

She closed the short distance between them, snagged him by the belt loop, and led him into the house. “Let’s go make up for Sunday night before supper. My friends issued an oral-sex challenge, and I picked you.”

CHAPTER EIGHT

She picked me.

Nelson stripped off his jeans and Jockeys in a single motion and kicked them toward the end table, where Scarlet's sweater and dress had landed a few seconds ago. Despite the lack of bra and panties in the pile, she was naked. All she wore was a wicked smile.

He tossed the plush blanket and throw pillows from the couch and recliner onto the carpet. "Might as well be comfortable."

Her grin widened and the look in her eyes promised he wouldn't give a damn about comfort in a minute or two. "Get comfy then. You're on the bottom."

"Don't I get a hello kiss first?" Not waiting for her answer, he slipped his hand around hers, tugged her closer, and touched his lips to hers. The feel of her skin against his torso and groin seduced him into returning for a real taste of the woman who brought out the adventurer in him and gave him hope that he could find true happiness in a romantic relationship.

She sighed into his mouth as their tongues met, melting

into his welcome. Her fingers threaded into his hair, and she eliminated what little space existed between them. Those simple actions set his body on fire.

A soft moan vibrated through his jaw when he cupped her butt cheek. The silky skin tempted him to lay her out on the floor and make passionate love to her, but that was dessert and this was the appetizer.

After another slow exploration of her mouth, he eased away and touched his forehead to hers. “Hi.”

“Hi.” Her breathy greeting sparked a moment of satisfaction. “I hope you’re that good with your tongue in other places.”

“I’ll do my best.” He nibbled a path from her jaw to the curve of her shoulder and then to the gentle slope of her breast, enjoying every inch he rediscovered since their quickie in her kitchen what seemed like forever ago and yesterday. Her nipples puckered tighter as he followed the deep valley between the exquisite mounds of flesh. “Three days a week isn’t often enough.”

She whimpered above him. “No renegotiating during sex. I can’t think straight.”

“Mm, that’s the point. I want to see and touch you every day.” He licked a ring around her rosy peak before flicking his tongue across the tip. Her shuddering gasp made his balls contract and his erection harden almost to the point of pain. “And give you orgasms. You’re so sexy, especially when you come.”

“Stop trying to talk me into things, and lie down on the blanket.” Her knees buckled when he sucked her nipple into his mouth, rendering her order too husky to sound bossy.

All the same, he released the tight bud, guided her to the floor, and stretched out on his back in front of her. “If I pass the oral test, will you agree to seven days a week?”

"Four." She knelt beside him and swung her leg past his head, narrowly missing his nose and putting her perfect ass right above his face.

The bird's eye view of her clit's hiding place and the sweet scent of her arousal drew his lips to her inner thigh. "Six."

"Five." Humid breath bathed his cock a moment before her mouth closed around him.

"Holy…" After her long thought-stealing suck, he popped free of her lips, leaving him aching for more. "God, I need more of your mouth. Seven."

She squeaked when he kissed the indentation at the top of her thigh, putting him less than an inch from her dark curls. "That's not how negotiation—"

A slow lick through her slick folds rewarded him with a drawn-out groan and her salty-sweet flavor. "You taste delicious. Seven."

Wet heat once again surrounded his dick, nearly distracting him from his target. Her body moved over him as she eased upward and then swallowed him whole. His eyes tried to roll back in his head with the overload of sensation spreading up his cock and through his balls, but he went in search of her clit instead of wallowing in the pleasure of his first blow job.

Determined to give as good as he got, he slid one hand along her ribs to play with her nipple and grasped her ass with the other. With every lick and flutter over the swollen nub, he rolled a taut bud between his thumb and finger. Her hums and moans vibrated through his erection, but he channeled every mind-numbing feeling into his effort to earn seven days a week.

She arched and rocked against his face, still mouth-fucking his dick like she couldn't get enough. He increased his pace until his tongue couldn't move and then sucked her clit between his teeth. Her legs trembled for several seconds before she grabbed his testicles and cried out around his about-to-blow cock.

He gave up the fight to slow his own release now that he'd delivered hers, letting the intensity of the moment sweep him over the edge. An unexpected growl escaped his throat, and his pulse pounded in his ears as a second stronger wave followed the first rush of heat up his length.

Deep physical satisfaction carried him away in a weightless cloud, but it didn't keep him from falling. Scarlet brought out emotions he hadn't expected to feel for a woman ever again after his farce of a marriage. She didn't hide anything from him, not her passion or amusement or annoyance. She was real, and this was how love was supposed to feel.

He shifted on the blanket, guiding her leg over him and meeting her halfway. More than anything, he wanted to hold her while their hearts slowed to a normal rhythm. As she settled against his chest, he kissed the top of her head. "Seven."

Her quiet laughter sounded so relaxed and genuine that he might be willing to budge on seven to have more than three days. "Five. I get together with friends twice a week for dinner, drinks, and dishing."

"Are these the same friends who issued the oral-sex challenge? Because I can work with that." He tipped her chin up and grinned at her. Her jaw sported a reddish patch, probably from his scruff, tempting him to check her upper thighs for more of the same. "They have some very good ideas."

"Yes, they do. One of them is Cerise, who will be a recipient of a challenge in the near future." She levered up on her elbow and her stomach made a rumbly noise. "Something smells really good. What's for supper?"

"Pulled pork sandwiches, baked potato wedges, and corn on the cob." Even though his legs were still a little rubbery and he would've preferred more cuddling, he rolled to his feet and offered her a hand up.

Studying him over her shoulder, Scarlet reached for the closest piece of clothing—his shirt—and then accepted his offer to help her stand. "If I have lunch with you on the sixth day, you have to agree to oral sex and cooking for me at least twice a week."

"Done." Careful to hide his elation, he led her to the arched opening opposite the couch. "You're welcome to use the bathroom in my bedroom if you need it. Down the hall. First door to the right. My daughter's in charge of keeping the other bathroom clean. I can't guarantee you'll make it in and out without getting lost in the dirty laundry."

Her smirk triggered a not-unwelcome warmth in his chest. "That's why I have a cleaning service come in every week. Housekeeping isn't one of my skillsets. I'm much better at building things and making messes. Back in a few minutes."

She sauntered toward the master bedroom as she slipped on his shirt, making him consider inviting her to stay the night. They had the house to themselves, but it would mean taking a serious step forward in their newly developing relationship. Scaring her off was the last thing he wanted to do after finding a woman who truly interested him. Besides, they both had to get up early for work in the morning. His fantasy included making love to her as they awoke and serving her breakfast in bed if she stayed.

Slow down. One step at a time.

He pulled on his jeans and headed to the kitchen to finish the last-minute menu details. Considering her easy acquiescence to upping their weekly date count, sexual satisfaction had already met or exceeded her expectations. His brain could focus on the best approach to sweeping her heart off its feet while he wooed her stomach with food.

HOPING TO CLEAR HER HEAD IN THE SPOTLESS BATHROOM, Scarlet splashed cool water on her face and, after a moment of consideration, she nixed the thought to rinse her mouth. Crème de la cock had been a tasty appetizer, certainly far more enjoyable than in the past. Mutual pleasuring had made all the difference in the world, and a subtle reminder seemed appropriate.

Oral abilities aside, Nelson couldn't possibly be as perfect as he seemed to be. So what if he knew exactly how to kiss her, lick her, touch her—and every other sex-related action—plus cook, clean, and carry on an intelligent conversation?

And let's not forget his negotiating skills and his interest in Mom and Dad's wellbeing.

She didn't regret agreeing to six-times-a-week date-sex, except that she would have to admit the truth to her friends and herself. Nelson Whitaker's body wasn't the only part of him she wanted. He was a nice guy worth getting to know better, if she could move past the trepidation.

How had that happened, especially after forty years of playing up her nerd card to keep people from thinking she was all boobs and no brain?

It doesn't have to get serious.

The mouthwatering aroma of slow-roasted pork nudged her from the bathroom and gave her something else to think about while she ignored the unexpected feelings rattling around inside her head and heart. Low expectations had been her default setting for a long time. How could it be anything else when her parents had the perfect marriage and most everyone else she knew didn't or hadn't?

A framed photo on the dresser caught her attention as she crossed the bedroom. Although the younger man holding a baby in one arm and a toddler on his knee wore the smile of someone less reserved than the Nelson she knew, his expression conveyed the same down-to-earth sincerity and kindness. Laugh lines crinkled the skin around his eyes and mouth when he forgot to be stuffy, and he obviously adored his kids. His smile had brightened during Sunday's blind date when he'd talked about them and the trials of raising teenagers as a single father. He hadn't offered their names, but pride had shone on his face each time he'd mentioned his son or his daughter.

Parenting agreed with him. Had she missed out on that experience?

She shook her head and continued to the living room. Her sentimentality extended to her parents and not much else. Commercials didn't make her cry, and the thought of watching a sappy movie was as appealing as swimming with eels. Did menopause destroy common-sense brain cells?

"Corn'll be ready in fifteen minutes." Nelson popped around the kitchen doorway, jeans and nothing else giving her an eyeful of bare-chested, barefooted man. He might not sport a six-pack, but he clearly worked out or did his fair share of physical labor. "Want a glass of wine? I picked up a bottle of what we had Sunday night at The Vinery on my way home from work."

Sexy and perfectly imperfect. She needed to keep her wits about her, or she'd end up more infatuated with him than she already was. "Let's wait until the food's ready. Can I help with anything?"

A hint of a smile played on his lips. "Sure. Come a little closer and I'll tell you what I need."

She raised an eyebrow at him and closed most of the distance between them. "I meant with cooking."

He skimmed his fingertips along the back of her thigh to the hem of his shirt. "Kissing and touching get things cooking, and I really enjoy creating heat with you."

"What if one of us gets burned?" The words snuck out of her mouth before her brain fully engaged, but she preferred acknowledging the truth and planning for the consequences to a face full of sand from burying her head.

His smirk slipped and the laugh lines disappeared. Locking his gaze on hers, he weaved his fingers between hers on both hands. "I've been burned worse than I thought I could survive. My wife didn't want to be married to me anymore, but instead of telling me, she left—with a guy she'd been cheating on me with for God knows how long. No divorce. No Dear John letter. Just gone. She died on her way to wherever they were going together. I found out the truth during the police investigation, and my kids discovered their mother chose her lover over them. It was rough. But I can't judge every woman by what she did. A leap of faith doesn't mean I'm jumping into a fire."

A lump formed in her throat and the tightness spread to her chest. She'd tried giving men the benefit of the doubt. Every damn time, they'd proven her wrong, enough times that she'd chosen her career instead of believing she could have the kind of relationship her parents had.

She swallowed, but it didn't help.

"Scarlet, I like you a lot, probably more than should be possible in the short time we've known each other." He lifted her hand to his mouth and pressed his lips to her knuckles. "I'm going to go way out on a limb here and say I think I'm falling in love with you. Being with you…has challenged everything I thought I knew about myself, but it feels so right."

"I, um…" Panic churned in her stomach with a dash of hope, chasing her appetite into hiding. Not much in her life could claim to have achieved that reaction before. She inhaled in an attempt to silence the faint buzzing in her ears. A slow exhale barely kept the room from pitching beneath her feet.

"Are you okay? You look a little pale." He scooped her into his arms, carried her to the couch, and cradled her on his lap. "I didn't mean to rush things. I'm usually much more circumspect, but you have this unexplainable impact on me."

She dropped her chin to her chest and closed her eyes, trying her damnedest to shake off the disconcerting lightheadedness. "It's fine. You feel what you feel. I just wasn't expecting…"

A long sigh all but confirmed he'd been hoping for a different response. "I wasn't, either. And I know this isn't going how you planned. The heart has a way of doing what it wants, like it or not."

His warm breaths tickled her legs in contrast to the slight draft across her bare bottom, inciting her stupid hormones again. Then her stomach rumbled, contradicting its earlier assertion that food was a bad idea.

He kissed her forehead and removed his arm from under her knees, ending the draft but putting the side of her thigh in direct contact with the distinguishable lump behind his zipper. "No matter what you decide about us, I'm still going to feed you."

His nurturing nature didn't irritate her as much as it should have, a testament to how far his declaration had thrown her off-balance. She took another deep breath and let it out slowly as she opened her eyes. Beeping saved her from having to fill the awkward silence. “Okay.”

He helped her to her feet and then walked her to the kitchen table. His quiet watchfulness almost made her wish she could tell him she liked his company, even if she didn’t want to analyze all the feelings swimming around in her menopausal brain.

Damn angsty drama. This is why I stopped dating thirty years ago.

The timer stopped its chirping, and the aroma of roasted corn filled the air when he opened the oven. Her belly growled repeatedly, clearly only caring about food. Maybe it had the right idea.

She leaned against the closest chair at the round wooden table to watch while he shucked the ears, set a baking sheet of golden-brown potato wedges on the stovetop, and placed a package of hoagie rolls next to the crockpot. His efficiency said he cooked often, probably most days since his late not quite ex-wife had vanished from his life.

Without turning toward her, he removed the lid from the crock and gestured at the dishes beside it with his elbow. “Go ahead and fill your plate while I get our drinks. Beer, wine, milk, juice, or water?”

His sudden casual-acquaintance aloofness spoke volumes about the emotional distance he’d put between them. It stung, but no leap of faith could scale that wall and she could hardly blame him for building it. Her own stood strong and tall.

As she stepped away from the table, he moved to the refrigerator several feet farther across the kitchen, sparking a twinge of guilt. “I’ll have whatever you’re having.”

He gave a curt nod. “Just water. Tap, filtered, ice, no ice?”

“Filtered. No ice please.” A little alcohol might numb the

dull ache in her throat, but it also tended to make her more susceptible to foolish choices and loose lips.

She piled pulled pork on a roll and squirted on a generous helping of barbecue sauce, biting her tongue to prevent a diarrheal explanation of her reasons for avoiding romantic relationships. The uncomfortable silence stretched on as she added potatoes and an ear of corn to her plate.

He finally sat across from her with his own sandwich and sides a few minutes later. After fiddling with his napkin and then his silverware, he rested his hands palms down on either side of his plate. His long tapered fingers drummed on the placemat for several seconds before they stilled. “I’m not going to pressure you into a step you’re not willing to take, but I also don’t want to give up the sexual side of our agreement. We can stick to three days a week if you want to. Exclusive partners is all I ask.”

His jaw tensed, like the concession pained him. Of course, the new proposition didn’t exactly feel like a reprieve. It would, however, buy her some time to adjust to riding on a damn rollercoaster. God, she’d hated them her entire life.

Lowering the potato she’d stabbed with her fork, she pinned a stare on him until he looked up at her. His expression remained closed off, hiding whatever he was thinking and feeling—not at all like the man who had driven her to the hospital or stayed with her mother. Her mind blanked, and the careful words she’d expected to use to let him down easy evaporated. “Exclusive. Three days a week. Okay.”

That was a good way to start the end, wasn’t it?

SURROUNDED BY NELSON’S WARM BODY TANGLED WITH HERS and the intoxicating scent of sex, Scarlet closed her eyes as her heartbeat returned to normal. She forced them open again so she wouldn't succumb to sleep. Staying all night in his bed would only make leaving more difficult for both of them. Forever had never been her intent, and pretending she understood the dynamics of relationships wouldn't change the inevitable outcome.

She didn't want to hurt him. Hell, she'd barely begun to develop friendships that didn't feel superficial. How could she navigate romantic love without unrealistically high or dangerously low expectations when she had no experience with it?

She'd always been nothing but an observer—with her parents, her classmates, her coworkers.

He released a deep breath and sank deeper into the mattress. Then his lips brushed her shoulder in a soft caress that would serve as the perfect goodbye.

Long minutes passed, and light rhythmic exhales feathered across her skin.

She forced her own breathing to slow for a count of two hundred before she dared to roll away from him. After another two hundred of stillness, she eased out from under the covers and tiptoed to the living room for her clothes.

Tears threatened as she slipped on her shoes in the garage, but she gently pulled the door into the house closed until it clicked. Leaving was her only option.

CHAPTER NINE

"Damn it." Scarlet plunked the battery-powered screwdriver on the workbench on the far side of her car's spot in the garage and stomped into the house.

Everything that could go wrong had gone wrong over the past two days. A part that should've been readily available locally had required a trip halfway across the state to retrieve, wasting most of a day that she should've been using for three oil changes, a brake job, and a radiator flush. Of course, she'd then had to work through the night to finish those and the carburetor replacement. Plus, her reading glasses had broken partway through the task, requiring a duct-tape repair at the bridge.

The lack of sleep hadn't bothered her. The long-ass drive to Dayton and back had, because it had allowed her mind to wander, to replay Tuesday's dinner at Nelson's house and the naked activities they'd pursued. At least it had given her a legitimate excuse not to spend more time with him.

He's probably in love with my boobs anyway, not me.

The thought didn't sit right, especially when she'd been the one to sneak out in the middle of the night, but romantic relationships weren't among her strengths. That particular skill hadn't made its way into her genetic code.

Mom and Dad used it all.

She huffed out an irritated breath when the spot in the broom closet that usually held double A batteries was empty. "Didn't I just buy a new pack?"

Movement out the kitchen window as she closed the door caught her attention. The all-terrain wheelchair she'd rented bumped along toward the woods, her mom riding in it and her dad walking beside it. They stopped at the A-frame swing they'd given her for a housewarming gift, and Kenny helped Katherine from the chair, accompanied her to the swing, and sat next to her with their hands linked on his lap.

A drop of moisture leaked from Scarlet's eye, and she slid her glasses into her hair to brush it away. An IQ of 135 and multiple college degrees would never help her achieve perfection in a relationship, not like they had.

She sighed again and marched to the key hook on her way back to the garage. A trip to her bedroom would be pointless since her vibrator's batteries had died this morning seconds from a much-needed orgasm that didn't come.

Keys and purse in hand, she tramped back out to the garage. The inclination to tell her parents she needed to run an errand sent her toward the door leading to the backyard. Her phone buzzed against her hip as she reached for the knob. "What now?"

The screen darkened before she managed to work it free from the side pocket of her coveralls. She left greasy thumb prints when she tapped in her passcode.

"Are you free tonight? I'm getting takeout on my way home from a job in Mantua. Dessert is you."

Her stomach and her heart battled for the title of most tangled in knots. Seeing Nelson again would only make things worse. Cold turkey was the way to go, even if she preferred it hot.

"Can't. Spending time with my parents since they'll be moving back home soon."

Several minutes passed, long enough for her to decide not to interrupt her mom and dad, for guilt to settle deep into her gut, and to climb behind the wheel of her SUV before her cell vibrated again.

"Tell Kenny and Katherine I said hi."

The curt response twisted her insides tighter, but she dropped her phone in the cupholder and backed out of the garage. Batteries had to suffice from now on, even if it meant no more real dicks.

HIS DAUGHTER HAD GRADUATED FROM HIGH SCHOOL FOUR hours ago. She now ate cake with her friends and roughly a hundred guests at Meg's house. His son slung his arm around her from behind and grinned as she laughed at something he said. They were adults, almost ready to face the world without him.

Nelson excused himself from the gathering near the makeshift DJ stand, feeling too dejected, rejected, and ejected to socialize with the other parents. His kids still needed and appreciated him, but the person he'd most wanted to invite to today's festivities had dumped him.

The moment of truth replayed in his mind for the four-hundredth time since he'd lain awake and pretended to sleep while Scarlet slipped from his bed at two in the morning without so much as a goodbye, let alone a kiss or a promise to see him soon. He'd made slow love to her for hours after their less-than-romantic dinner, in the hope she would see how good they were together. It had morphed into a long and desperate farewell rather than the beautiful expression of love he'd intended.

He wandered toward the stock tank filled with ice and bottled drinks, fighting the urge to check his phone. Scarlet had bailed on him twice when he'd suggested they hook up on Thursday and again on Friday. Her excuses—driving to Dayton for an engine part and spending time with her parents—might or might not have been legitimate, but they made her plans crystal clear.

She didn't want him anymore, not after he'd been honest with her about his feelings. He had pushed too hard and fallen too fast.

As he twisted open a bottle of water and continued a slow walk along the fence line, a black and white cow mooed a few yards away, its melancholy timbre summing up his mood. Considering the partially swollen udder visible at the rear legs, he made a fairly reliable assumption about her bovine gender. "Right there with you, Bessie."

A familiar-sounding squeal pulled his attention back to the party on the far side of the mown field. Em's purple baseball cap stood out at the buffet table and her voice carried over the background conversation. "You came!"

The knot in his stomach tightened. That kind of excitement from his daughter meant she'd gained a new boyfriend—*Please, no*—or a favorite teacher had shown up. Whichever guest she'd greeted hid among the line of teenagers working on second and third helpings of dessert.

He sighed and headed toward the group, determined to be polite in spite of his moroseness.

The crowd broke apart as he passed the drink supply, giving him a clear view of the new arrival. His heart climbed to his Adam's apple and stuck there.

Scarlet faced Em with a wrapped gift tucked under one arm. Jeans, a baggy t-shirt, and work boots did nothing to disguise her shapely silhouette, not that he wouldn't recognize her anywhere.

This day just keeps getting better and better.

He ducked toward a wall of people watching the cornhole tournament, but his daughter waved both hands in the air before he reached his hiding place. "Dad, come here! I want you to meet somebody!"

Met her, fell in love with her, and got dumped by her. I don't need a damn introduction. I want her to give us a chance.

Wishing he'd snuck a flask of Jim Beam into the party like a rebellious eighteen-year-old, he stiffened his spine and marched to the woman who had broken his heart. With a plastered-on fake smile, he held out his hand. "Nelson Whitaker. Emily's dad."

Her lips, lips he'd kissed and dreamed about, stretched into a thin line as her eyes narrowed, suggesting she hadn't known he was Em's father. She cleared her throat and opened her mouth as if to speak, but nothing came out.

"Dad, this is Ms. Brinks. You know, the lady who, um, talked to me about being an electrician." His daughter's gaze ping-ponged back and forth between Scarlet and him. Hero worship shone in her expression as she practically bounced out of her flip-flops. "Remember I told you she owns the auto repair shop down the road? And she used to be an engineer at NASA?"

Scarlet glanced toward his outstretched hand and then up to about chest level. Did she feel guilty for disappearing without an explanation?

Ghosting—that's what his kids called it. The only difference was she'd all but told him to get lost by text message.

He withdrew his hand and slid it into the front pocket of khakis. "Of course. I also remember she helped you apply to the apprenticeship program."

"Dad, you're not going to make a big deal about that, are you?" Emily drilled a stare into him, clearly willing him not to make a scene. "I asked her to help me."

"Do I ever make a big deal out of anything?" The truth got no reaction out of his former lover or his daughter. Ready to put an end to the charade, he gave Em a quick peck on the cheek and tugged his keys free. Paperwork and brooding awaited him. "I'm proud of you. Text me when you're heading home in the morning, okay?"

She frowned. "Okay."

As he turned toward the rows of cars parked at the edge of the field, he spared a quick look at the woman who had followed in Kelly's footsteps by unceremoniously dumping him. "Enjoy the party, Ms. Brinks."

Despite the feeling of someone watching him on the walk to his truck, he didn't slow or stray from the shortest path to his parking spot. Scarlet hadn't spoken a word or shaken his hand, so he obviously no longer existed in her mind. Avoidance had been her way of pretending they didn't know each other.

He climbed behind the wheel with an ache that rivaled the one he'd experienced after finding out his wife didn't give a damn about him, either. "I sure know how to pick 'em."

STUFFING A BITE OF CAKE IN HER MOUTH, SCARLET FOUGHT the irrational urge to follow Nelson—Emily the pizza delivery person's father, Emily the lawn-mowing girl's dad—and tell him everything she hadn't said during their introduction by his daughter. She couldn't exactly blame him for acting like he'd never met her. He hadn't made a big deal out of her leaving in the middle of the night while he slept or creating reasons not to get together again, even though she probably deserved it. Making a public spectacle of himself or anyone else wasn't his style.

No, Nelson Whitaker preferred to suffer in silence.

"Sorry about that." Emily grimaced and glanced toward the makeshift parking lot. "My dad's been—"

"Scarlet! You finally made it." Rose popped around Nelson's daughter, her scalp beneath the freshly buzzed side of her head catching the early evening sunlight. "Did you find Meg yet?"

Scarlet washed down the sugary goodness with a swallow of iced tea. "I was just about—"

"Your name's Scarlet?" Wide eyes and a grin accompanied Emily's whispered question. "Like phone-sex Scarlet? Oh my gosh, this is too awesome. You and my dad are dating?"

The heat of a thousand white dwarf stars swept up Scarlet's neck and across her cheeks, not a good mix with the sick feeling in her heart and buttercream frosting lodged somewhere between her mouth and her stomach.

Rose snorted and wrapped her arm around Scarlet's shoulders. "You should see your face, Scar. No, Emmie, they aren't dating, because this fool is too scared to admit she's in love with your father. The way she's been moping around since she dumped him is pathetic."

Perching her hands on her hips, the young woman glared at Scarlet. "You dumped my dad?"

Guilt amplified the nausea, but deflecting with a phone-sex-Rose comment didn't seem like a good idea. Nobody was allowed to know about that, and it didn't have quite the same cadence as phone-sex Scarlet. “It’s for the best. I don’t want to hurt him.”

“Too late. You already did.” Emily huffed out a sigh. “Besides, why would you hurt him if you’re in love with him? That doesn’t make sense. It’s like making a cake and then throwing it away so you won’t eat it.”

“She’s right, you know.” Rose’s two cents came as Poppy, Sienna, and Meg joined them.

The owner of Whacked crossed her arms in front of her, pushing up her cleavage and revealing the edge of what looked like a sword tattoo. “Who’s throwing away cake? If you don’t want it, give it to me. Damn PMS.”

Still giving Scarlet the evil eye, Emily snatched away her plate and handed it to Sienna. “Here. Can someone please explain to me why falling in love is a bad thing? Especially when you know the other person feels the same way? It doesn’t compute.”

“You stole my cake!” Focusing on that part of the conversation was far easier than trying to explain why she’d had no choice but to hurt Nelson. Didn’t anybody see how high her parents had set the bar with their perfect marriage? And that offering him the one thing men wanted from her had been payback for all the jerks who had never looked beyond her boobs?

“Oh, you want it back? Here you go.” Em grabbed the chunk of remaining cake and smashed it in Scarlet’s face. “That’s for breaking my dad’s heart.”

As punishments went, marble cake topped with blue and white icing up her nose and in her eyes hardly fit the crime. She blinked to clear the gooey frosting from her eyelashes. “Do you think mine feels any better?”

Not waiting for a response, she stalked away, glad for the mess that would hide the ridiculous saltwater leaking from her stinging eyes. Love's illogical tendencies made an excellent backup reason for ending things now. Hearts were unreliable most of the time and too fragile all of the time.

"Scarlet? What happened to you?" Her mother's voice came from beyond the limited view of frosting and cake crumbs.

"I got in a fight with a piece of cake." She scooped the mess out of her eye sockets with the hem of her t-shirt. Luckily, the stupid tears went with it. "What're you doing here, Mom? Aren't you supposed to be home resting?"

Her dad's frown greeted her when she finally removed enough goo to see. "Bell's a small town. You think you're the only person Emily delivers pizza to? Besides, the doctor cleared your mother for normal activity four days ago. And don't start on me, young lady. My ankle is fine."

A glob of frosting fell from her shirt and splatted on the toe of her boot. She stomped once, sending it flying into the grass. "I haven't lived in town since I was eighteen. How would I know who orders pizza? I'm just trying to take care—"

"We're not senile yet, so stop trying to be the boss of us." He shook his head, wearing the same irritated expression from a few days ago when he'd asked about inviting Nelson to the thank-you dinner they'd never gotten around to having. "Seems to me you should be paying more attention to your own life."

"What's that supposed to mean?" She wished the words back as soon as they left her mouth, mostly because he wouldn't have any qualms about telling her exactly what he meant. "Never mind. I need to go home and wash my face so I can finish a brake job."

Her mom's hand closed over her forearm before she managed a step toward the lines of vehicles less than a hundred feet away. "It's okay to have doubts about your relationship with Nelson, Lettie, but don't give up when things start to get difficult. It's obvious you two have feelings for each other, and don't bother to deny it. If you had an argument, talk it out. You can do your best to save your relationship or you can have regrets. I don't recommend regrets."

Pressing her lips together, Scarlet swallowed against the ache in her throat. "Regrets? You and Dad have always had the perfect marriage. I don't even know how to date, let alone navigate a serious relationship. And marriage? Why would I set myself up for that kind of failure?"

"There's no such thing as perfect." Her mother looked toward the man she'd married fifty-five years ago. "Your father and I separated for three months during your first year of grad school."

"*What?* No way." A quick study of her parents' pained gazes confirmed what she never would've believed. "But you… You're practically inseparable. And you always look so happy together."

Her dad tucked her mom's hand in his. "Because we almost lost each other. My biggest regret is that I can't ever get those days back. If you care about Nelson, you need to give yourself a boot in the backside and tell him. Take a chance. You've faced down every challenge your entire life. Don't turn into a quitter now."

Scarlet could only stare at her parents, the two people in the world who exuded more love and happiness than any couple she'd ever known. How had she missed seeing the divide that had happened? What would they have done if they hadn't had the strength and determination to save their marriage?

"Well, what are you waiting for?" Her mother snapped her fingers twice and shooed her away. "Go get your man!"

The urging from her mom and being called a quitter by her dad propelled Scarlet to the farthest parking space at the edge of the field, but doubts hit half a mile down the road from Rose's little farm. Putting her heart on the line and losing came with a significantly more painful set of consequences than getting a B in a class or failing to earn a promotion.

She detoured along the backroads instead of continuing into town to "get her man." Going for a drive had always cleared her head and helped her refocus.

Thirty miles later, she started another lap around the five-mile block where she'd learned to drive, no closer to negotiating an agreement between her heart and her brain.

CHAPTER TEN

LEANING BACK IN HIS DESK CHAIR, NELSON KNEADED HIS tight neck muscles and sighed. The first invoice still filled his computer screen, despite multiple attempts to add the client's name, contact information, and the amount due in the last half hour. Scarlet's expressionless face had superimposed itself on the form, refusing to let him work.

He pushed out of the chair and trudged along the dim hallway. The utter silence added to his moodiness. "Better get used to it."

Headlights flashed through the living room window, but he continued to the fridge for a change of scenery. Milk, juice, half a dozen kinds of cheese, two slices of stale pizza, and a bottle of ketchup didn't tempt him, so he opened the pantry. Another carryout meal held no appeal.

The doorbell rang as he reached for the Shredded Wheat. "Go away."

He nearly tossed the box over his shoulder for the lack of resistance. Why the hell had someone put an empty box back on the shelf?

Yes, he'd done it since he was the only person in the

house who ate cereal without the sugar content of a box of glazed donuts.

The chimes sounded again.

"Fine, I'll answer the damn door, but you better not be selling anything unless it's a fully cooked meal. Or Girl Scout cookies. I could go for some Thin Mints." He plunked the cereal box on the counter and headed for the living room.

Not bothering with a peek through the window, he turned the lock and swung open the door. Smears of blue and white covered most of the person's face, but the rest was all Scarlet—albeit with splotches of paint or something else dotting her clothes. His pulse skittered into an erratic beat throughout his body.

She glanced up at him and then down toward her feet. "Can I come in?"

He stepped aside, hoping she wasn't here to rake his feelings over the coals a second time, and gestured for her to enter. "What happened?"

Her brief hesitation soothed his own anxiety a tiny bit. Bending over, she untied the laces of her messier than usual boots. "Emily smashed a piece of cake in my face for breaking your heart."

A chuckle tried to sneak past his lips at the image that easily formed in his mind. His daughter tended to act first and think later in matters of fairness. "It looks like it ended up on more than just your face. I can see if I can find some clean clothes for you if you want to wash up. Em's a little taller, but a pair of her sweatpants should fit."

She sighed as she straightened. "There you go, being all nice and helpful after I treated you like crap. You're allowed to be hurt and angry. You should be."

"Hurt? Yes. Angry? No." Keeping his attention on the sticky-looking mask on her cheeks, he willed his heart and head not to read too much into her words. "Your feelings are as important as mine."

"See? There you go again." She tugged her shirt over her head, leaving her in a plain white bra. Her jeans landed on her boots a few seconds later. "You're too nice, Nelson."

And you're too close to being naked.

Averting his gaze, he forced three calming breaths to try to control his dick's automatic reaction to her. "You can use my bathroom. I'll go look for some clothes."

Her barely audible footsteps followed him across the living room. "What if— Never mind."

What had she meant to say? Was she here for sex? Or something more?

Shoving speculation deep into his gut, he let her comment go. "I'll leave the clothes on my dresser. Are you hungry? Or thirsty?"

She stopped at the entrance to the hall. "Got any Jack? For courage."

The floodgates collapsed, freeing his hopes and feeding his dreams. He pivoted toward her. "You don't have to be brave with me."

Her lower lip trembled and she blinked her frosting-coated lashes. A hint of uncertainty shone through her seriousness. "So… I'm sorry for the way I left in the middle of the night. It's no better than what your wife did. God, you should be so pissed off at me for doing that. The thing is…I might be falling in love with you. And it scares the hell out of me because I want you to be happy too. Months and years from now. Pretty much forever. Is that how this feeling is supposed to work?"

Hell, if he knew. Happily-ever-after had eluded him the first time around, despite his best effort.

He took a step closer and cradled her jaw in his palm,

about to choke on the rush of hope through his heart and soul. Words refused to form as emotion filled every part of him. A simple touch of his lips to hers urged him to return for another taste of sweetness—more from her honesty than the icing or the cake. He poured everything into the next kiss, determined to convince her he felt the same and that they could work on the forever part together.

Her breath warmed his chin as she eased away and rested her forehead against his. "I'll take that as a yes, I think. Can we skip the clothes? Maybe call this a done deal and start over?"

He scooped her into his arms and carried her toward the bathroom. "I'm sorry too. I tried to go faster than you were ready for, and it backfired. Three days a week? Five?"

She nibbled a path from his ear to his mouth. "Seven would be better, and I want more than sex."

"What about your twice-a-week get-togethers with—"

A door banged shut somewhere on the other side of the house.

"Hey, Dad! Where are you?" Rapid footsteps accompanied his daughter's voice. "You got a minute?"

He lowered Scarlet's feet to the floor and leaned in to whisper in her ear. "Bathroom. Hurry."

Before the mostly naked woman in his bedroom took a step, Em appeared in the doorway. "There you— What's she doing here? And why isn't she wearing any clothes?"

Stepping in front of Scarlet, he frowned. "They were covered in cake crumbs and frosting. Any idea how that might have happened?"

"She deserved it for dumping you." Emily crossed her arms and glared past him. The only thing missing from Emily's response was the foot stomp that had always accompanied her little-girl tantrums.

"That's for me to decide." His hand connected with bare skin as he reached behind him, setting his heart pounding once again and messing with his ability to focus on the conversation. "Um, we're working on figuring out what we want, you know, like adults. Why are you here instead of at the party?"

A pout replaced the glare. "You seemed upset, and I was worried about you. Grownups aren't supposed to do the stupid boyfriend-girlfriend high-school drama stuff. Breaking up and getting back together fifteen times. Why do you think I'd rather hang out with my friends than play musical chairs with boys?"

He locked his gaze on her to keep from rolling his eyes. "It was one time, and adults are people too. We have baggage and issues and complicated feelings. Fortunately, Scarlet and I are on the same page now, so I think you need to apologize for smashing cake in her face on my behalf."

Em pursed her lips, clearly weighing all the evidence. "Fine. I'm sorry, Ms. Brinks. But no more freaking out, guys. Either of you. Got it?"

Slipping her fingers through his, Scarlet peeked around him. "Okay."

Her touch incited tingles in places he wanted to share with her in private. "Yes, we're good. Why don't you head back to Meg's so we can kiss and make up?"

His daughter scoffed as she turned toward the hall. "Kiss, huh? Understatement of the century, most likely. Don't forget to use a condom."

Heat flashed across his cheeks, but it traveled much lower when Scarlet burst out laughing beside him. The joyful sound warmed him from the inside out.

The love of his life grinned at him and winked. "No

worries, Emily. He has most of a box in the nightstand drawer."

A choked laugh came from the direction of the living room. "I'm not asking how you know that. Oh, I'll give you plenty of warning before I come home from Meg's in the morning."

A few seconds later, a door banged closed.

He tugged Scarlet into his arms, glad to have her to himself again. "Will you stay with me tonight?"

She unfastened the top button of his shirt and started on the next one before looking up at him. Her smile softened to match the trust in her eyes. "That sounds like a good start."

Are you ready for the next story in the Romancing the Phone series? Get *Smooth Operator*!

Thanks for reading! If you enjoyed this story, please consider leaving a review on the retailer's website, BookBub, and/or Goodreads to help other readers find their next book! Join my Facebook reader group for fun discussions and subscribe to my newsletter to receive the latest news about releases, sales, book signings, and more.

SMOOTH OPERATOR SNEAK PEEK

Chapter 1

Barton Holloway scratched at eight days' worth of beard stubble on his neck and then flipped on his turn signal for the next driveway. The lane led toward a white farmhouse set in the middle of a stand of massive oak trees, his single headlight illuminating the leaf-strewn gravel in the quickly approaching dusk.

Rose Chambers. Owner of Bell Lumber.

She would be interviewing him for the delivery driver job at her lumberyard.

He'd once had a crush on a girl named Rose in high school—long before his pair of short-lived marriages. The image of the leggy young woman with long brown hair, brown eyes, and glasses formed in his mind. He smiled, warmed by the memory. God, he missed being fourteen and not having a care in the world, other than attracting the attention of the gorgeous troublemaker four years his senior.

Rosie Kovac. I wonder where she is now.

Hopefully, this Rose would give him the opportunity to switch from long-haul driving to local deliveries. His back would sure appreciate the change. Nearly three decades of sitting behind the wheel of a big rig had taken its toll on his forty-six-year-old body.

He shut off the purring engine of his rebuilt Harley, took off his helmet, and downed the dregs of the convenience-store coffee from his insulated mug. A shudder rippled through him at the bitter aftertaste, but he shook it off. His interview took precedence over a twelve-hour nap after more than a week on the road.

Returning the mug to its holder, he engaged the kickstand and swung his leg over the seat. His legs protested the walk to the wraparound porch and the short climb up the three steps. At least the pinched nerve in his left hip wasn't to blame. Nope, this time the culprit was the combination of roughly six thousand miles in a week, the damp fall weather, and an old football injury.

Middle age sucks.

Despite being fifteen minutes early for their Saturday evening appointment, he pulled in a chilly breath and raised his fist to knock on the side door—the one Ms. Chambers, possibly his future employer, had directed him to use in her email.

Before he made contact, a husky feminine groan carried through what looked to be a partially opened window a few feet to the left of the door. "I love the feel of your balls in my hand. Do you want me to squeeze them? How about if I eat your cock and swallow it whole? I want to suck it while Ella licks my clit."

A threesome?

A hint of interest flickered behind Barton's zipper, waking

him up faster than the high-octane coffee he'd chugged. Of course, jacking off to the free girl-on-girl-on-guy porn soundtrack right then and there wasn't exactly an option. Too bad his last attempt at a relationship had resulted in getting dumped about three or four years ago, because real sex would hit the spot better than going solo again.

Another reason forty-six bites.

"Yeah, just like that, baby. Mmm. Oh, that feels so good." Her sexy voice sounded closer, maybe right on the other side of the glass. She moaned again, and sucking noises joined in the fuck fest.

When he retreated a step to go wait by his bike, movement in the window caught his attention. A backlit pair of hands wrapped around a rigid dick-shaped appendage beyond the thin curtains moved up and down in a steady motion. The sucking sounds continued, along with some heavy panting and several breathy sighs, even though no mouth covered the head of the stiff cock. Was it from Ella going down on his kinky boss-to-be?

"Play with my nipples, Kip. God, I'm so close. Oh. Oh. Oh. Yes! I'm coming, Ella! Now! Oh, God! Yes!"

Keening carried to Barton's ears, and he clenched his jaw to keep from groaning with her. While he enjoyed porn as much as the next guy, voyeurism had never been on his radar. The woman had a sexy as hell voice, all low and smooth and husky, like a shot of aged whiskey gliding down his throat. Damn, he needed a cigarette, and he didn't even smoke.

No other orgasmic noises followed, which seemed a little weird, considering her steady pumping on the rod in her grip. "I hope that was as good for you as it was for me. Same time next week? Okay. Have an awesome night, Kip."

The sucking suddenly ended, and a gurgle and slurp followed.

"About fucking time you unplugged, stupid sink." The business end of a plunger appeared for a moment before she plunked it into a now-visible bucket on what was probably a counter. "I hope you enjoyed getting sucked off as much as Kip."

Barton slapped his hand over his mouth to hold in a laugh, but he only succeeded in creating a massive fart impersonation.

"Who's out there?" His no-longer-future employer whipped back the curtain and pressed her cheek against the bug screen. Her thick-framed glasses tilted, leaving them crooked across her nose and eyes, but she stared right at him. "Shit. You're here for the job interview, aren't you? You're early. I can explain, but I'm not going to. Give me a sec."

He bit down on his lower lip to keep from grinning. At least the woman owned her behavior and didn't give a damn if anyone approved or disapproved. "Take your time."

After the bang of what sounded like a cabinet closing and then faint footsteps, the door swung inward, revealing a tallish woman in baggy overalls and work boots. One strap hung down to her hip and half the bib draped across her right breast. A pert nipple poked at her flannel shirt, hinting that she might not be wearing a bra.

A perfect breast. Not too big. Not too small. Just right.

He lifted his gaze to her face as she raised the eyebrow that wasn't half hidden by a thick fall of glossy brown hair. Despite his dick swelling behind his zipper again and being caught checking her out, he offered his hand. "Ms. Chambers? Barton Holloway."

She narrowed her eyes as she met his grip with an equally firm one. Then she gestured for him to enter and led him into the room with the window—the kitchen. "Call me Rose. If you repeat any of what you overheard or speculate about it, your ass is fired. Understood?"

"Sure, but I didn't know you hired me yet." He sat in the chair she indicated, not sure whether to celebrate his new job or quit. "Maybe you should tell me more about what I'll be doing."

Leaning her hip against the counter, she crossed her arms under her attention-grabbing breasts. "Loading and unloading lumber. Standard sizes up to sixteen feet long. Plywood. Trusses. You'll be making local deliveries within twenty-five miles. Ninety percent of my customers are builders and contractors, so you'll have multiple large orders per day. Can you handle a forklift?"

He nodded and forced his eyes to stay focused on her neck and above. "Yep."

Her expression didn't change. "How about a flatbed truck? Do you know anything about repairs and maintenance on Freightliner diesel engines?"

"I can drive flatbeds, dump trucks, eighteen-wheelers, and pretty much every other kind of truck, car, and bike. Manual and automatic." He rested his elbows on the table, still studying her unreadable face. What kind of business owner hired a person and conducted the job interview after the fact? "I've done most of my own repairs on the rigs I've driven for going on twenty years. I also worked in my grandpa's repair shop before I got my CDL."

She picked up a folder from the counter, crossed to where he sat, and set the file in front of him. "That's why I'm hiring you. It's time to discuss wages and fill out the paperwork. The background check came back clear, but you'll need to take a drug test since you'll be operating heavy equipment. I can't afford a lawsuit or damages. Starting salary is in the offer letter."

"You're thorough. I'll give you that. And decisive." He flipped open the folder. "Got a—"

"Right here." In a single smooth motion, she unclipped a pen from her bib pocket and handed it to him. "Take your time reading everything. I'd rather not have to fill the job again for at least a few years. Can I get you a glass of water or some iced tea? Unsweet."

"I'm good, thanks." Despite her voice still strumming his nerve endings, he picked up the top page of the half dozen or so papers. The letters blurred until he straightened his arm and blinked twice.

"How about a pair of reading glasses?" Her visible eyebrow rose again as she reached for the overflowing basket on the counter. The change in her profile lit a spark in his belly as she gave him a clear view of the nearly shaved side of her head and a heart-shaped birthmark below her ear.

"No way." The whispered reaction spilled out of his mouth before his brain fully engaged.

She frowned at him over her shoulder, but the lack of a ring on her left hand as her fingers closed around a pair of glasses made the spark flare. "Denial doesn't prevent the need to magnify the fine print."

The pen slipped from his grip and clattered on the table. "Rosie Kovac?"

Her frown deepened. "How do you know my maiden name?"

"I think my ego just shriveled up and died." He leaned back in the chair and chuckled. "Barton Holloway. I asked you to the homecoming dance when you were a senior and I was a freshman. You said I was too young for you."

She lifted her hand to her mouth as her eyes widened, and her cheeks flushed the color of the pink carnations his grandmother had grown in her flower garden. "Bart? Oh my God.

Everybody called you Simpson because you always had a crew cut that looked like— I'm sure you remember well enough without me reminding you. Your hair is longer now. And the beard. You're a lot better looking than Bart Simpson as an adult. Maybe I should've said yes."

A belly laugh rumbled out of him, the first of its kind for a long time, and he swiped at his watering eyes. "You definitely should've. I had it so bad for you."

A wide smile spread across her face, reaching her pretty brown eyes.

Finally in control of his laughter, he returned her grin. "Your hair's a lot shorter now, but I like it. It fits the girl I knew back then."

"Thank you." She shoved the long side away from her cheek and lifted her chin. "My daughter thinks I'm trying to relive my youth."

His insides twisted unexpectedly. "So, you're married?"

"God, no." Her expression morphed into a reflection of pure horror. "Divorced. For a long time. You?"

"Divorced." He shrugged, not sure why that fact still bothered him. He sure as hell didn't have feelings for either of his ex-wives, unless he counted disgust. "Twice. Six years since the second one."

She closed the short distance to the table and sat across from him. "That's rough. Was it because you were on the road a lot? Some people need a lot of attention."

"Indirectly, I suppose. They both liked when I was gone. It made keeping a boyfriend on the side easier." The admission drew a scowl from Rose, but he rubbed his palms on his jeans instead of reaching to smooth away the anger lines around her mouth. "The worst part was asking my doctor to test me twice. You can't be too careful, even when you've been using protection all the time, but that was humiliating."

"I can only imagine. My ex was just a shitty husband and a shittier father. Always shirking his responsibilities. Never showing up for Beau's and Meg's birthdays and school events. He still—" She shook her head, making her hair fall across her cheek again. "Never mind. I'm sure you don't want to hear me rant about delinquent child support and non-parenting."

"I'm sorry. He sounds like a real loser." Barton picked up the pen again and tapped it against the file. "How old are your kids?"

"Twenty and eighteen. Meg's a freshman at Miami of Ohio and Beau's a junior at Ohio State." Rose's sudden smile seemed to hold a bit of wistfulness. "I'm an empty-nester most of the time now. Of course, that means I can have wild parties at my house any time I want."

Unable to contain his grin, he chuckled. "Still getting into trouble, huh?"

"Causing trouble, you mean." She waggled her eyebrows and snorted. "I have too many bills and too much work to do to be the instigator anymore. At least Beau has a part-time job that helps cover his tuition and Meg has three scholarships. Trying to keep the farm going and running the lumberyard, on top of paying for their housing? I need you to take the delivery driver job so I don't have to try to find time to do it. Plus, it doesn't gain me anything by trading a salary that's in the budget for exhaustion and the possibility of late deliveries. I can't lose those accounts."

Determined to make both their lives a little easier, he donned the too-small reading glasses she'd set on the table and focused on the paper in his hand again. "Unless the pay sucks, I want the job. Between the aches and pains I already had and the new ones that keep appearing out of nowhere, my body can't take eighteen hours a day on the road anymore. Getting old is for the birds."

"Speak for yourself. Maybe you're old, but I'm not." The teasing in her sexy voice made his heart pitter-patter and his dick harden like it was thirty years younger.

He didn't dare glance up and risk letting her see the same infatuation he'd suffered from in high school. "I doubt you'll ever be old. Give me a few minutes to read through everything and fill out the paperwork. You don't happen to know of any local apartments or duplexes for rent, do you? Or a cheap house for sale that I can fix up?"

"Not much in the way of rentals in Bell, but I can ask around about fixer-uppers." Her chair screeched on the hardwood floor and then he caught movement out of the corner of his eye as she rose. "I'll check the real estate listings while you finish."

"Thanks." Silence surrounded him as he read and signed the contract and forms, but it wasn't uncomfortable. Her presence permeated his skin, soothing the muscle twinges and exhaustion. The long-forgotten flame obviously hadn't burned itself out, despite all the time that had passed and the experiences that had made him weary and wary of women.

Unfortunately, she was now his boss. Fortunately, he would now spend his nights at home rather than on the road, even if he'd rather spend them with this all-too-intriguing incarnation of his dream girl.

Get *Smooth Operator*!

ABOUT THE AUTHOR

Mellanie Szereto is the *USA Today* Bestselling Author of over sixty romcoms and contemporary romances, most with characters who have plenty of life experience like herself. Whether you call them older, seasoned, mature, experienced, or later-in-life protagonists, they deserve love too! Her stories are often set in small towns with quirky main characters, fun secondary casts, and lots of humor. She enjoys gardening, cooking, and baking—as well as hiking to work off the fruits of her labor—and incorporates food into all of her stories. She lives in an old farmhouse in rural Indiana with her husband of thirty-eight years.

Visit her website for more information about her books!